still alive

(a lily dawn fbi suspense thriller—book 1)

ava strong

Ava Strong

Ava Strong is author of the REMI LAURENT mystery series, comprising six books (and counting); of the ILSE BECK mystery series, comprising seven books (and counting); of the STELLA FALL psychological suspense thriller series, comprising six books (and counting); of the DAKOTA STEELE FBI suspense thriller series, comprising six books (and counting); and of the LILY DAWN suspense thriller series, comprising five books (and counting).

An avid reader and lifelong fan of the mystery and thriller genres, Ava loves to hear from you, so please feel free to visit www.avastrongauthor.com to learn more and stay in touch.

ISBN: 978-1-0943-3029-7

BOOKS BY AVA STRONG

LILY DAWN FBI SUSPENSE THRILLER
STILL ALIVE (Book #1)
STILL HOPE (Book #2)
STILL AWAKE (Book #3)
STILL HERE (Book #4)
STILL MAD (Book #5)

REMI LAURENT FBI SUSPENSE THRILLER
THE DEATH CODE (Book #1)
THE MURDER CODE (Book #2)
THE MALICE CODE (Book #3)
THE VENGEANCE CODE (Book #4)
THE DECEPTION CODE (Book #5)
THE SEDUCTION CODE (Book #6)

ILSE BECK FBI SUSPENSE THRILLER
NOT LIKE US (Book #1)
NOT LIKE HE SEEMED (Book #2)
NOT LIKE YESTERDAY (Book #3)
NOT LIKE THIS (Book #4)
NOT LIKE SHE THOUGHT (Book #5)
NOT LIKE BEFORE (Book #6)
NOT LIKE NORMAL (Book #7)

STELLA FALL PSYCHOLOGICAL SUSPENSE THRILLER
HIS OTHER WIFE (Book #1)
HIS OTHER LIE (Book #2)
HIS OTHER SECRET (Book #3)
HIS OTHER MISTRESS (Book #4)
HIS OTHER LIFE (Book #5)
HIS OTHER TRUTH (Book #6)

DAKOTA STEELE FBI SUSPENSE THRILLER
WITHOUT MERCY (Book #1)
WITHOUT REMORSE (Book #2)
WITHOUT A PAST (Book #3)
WITHOUT PITY (Book #4)
WITHOUT HOPE (Book #5)

CHAPTER ONE

Lauren clung to the handle of the water ski, feeling her legs loose and wobbly beneath her. In front of her, the boat soared through the crystal blue water, and Lauren looked down to see her feet each on a ski. She'd never done this before, and she couldn't help but tremble as she imagined a shark leaping up and sinking his teeth into her chest.

She closed her eyes and let the adrenaline rush in. *You're okay. You can do this.*

When she opened her eyes, she was met by a sunny sky and the clear blue ocean. Behind her, the islands of the Bahamas were close. *I'm okay*, Lauren reminded herself.

"You've got this, Lauren!" On the deck of the boat, her best friend, Amy, was waving.

She was wearing a bright blue bikini, and Lauren couldn't help but laugh when she saw the bikini bottoms had a picture of a shark on them. Lifting her head, she nodded back—just as the boat hit a wave. *Crap! Don't lose your balance!*

Lauren pushed off hard on the skis, and the world went silent. Then she slapped back down on the surface of the water, water lapping at her face, pulling her hair back with its weight. The strength of the wind blew through her hair and whipped it back, and she opened her eyes and stared at the ice-blue sky. For a moment, she was weightless, lifted between two worlds. She might as well have just been flying. Lauren couldn't believe it. The wind felt like something alive, like a living thing had passed her by and breathed on her, lifting her from herself for a moment before dropping her back in this world with a splash of cold water.

She was steady.

Her heart was pounding, but as the next wave hit with a foamy hiss, she realized that she loved this.

"This is awesome!" Amy's boyfriend, Chad, was shouting. "You're on a speedboat! We're going to catch some tuna! Woohoo!"

As Chad's enthusiasm washed over her, Lauren felt her own excitement grow. She looked over at her boyfriend, Tom, who was steering the boat. He smiled and winked at her. Slowly, she relaxed a little.

This is going to be fine, she thought. *This is going to be fun!*

The boat was now at full throttle, and Amy and Chad were leaning against the railing, watching the waves. Adrenaline rushed through Lauren as the speed picked up, bringing her with it. She felt like she was the shark now, gliding at sea.

"Tom!" Lauren shouted. "I've got this! This is awesome!" Her words were whipped away by the wind, so only Tom could hear them.

Tom smiled. "I know," he said. "You're amazing."

Lauren smiled back. It was times like these that she thought maybe she was made for sports.

Just then, the boat hit a bump—a bump Lauren wasn't prepared for. The boat jerked, causing the table holding Lauren's water ski to jolt with it.

"Whoa!" Lauren yelled as her ski slipped from under her, and she found herself falling. She gasped as her body hit the water and dragged her under. The freezing water stole her breath. Struggling against the waves, Lauren's head burst out of the water as she gasped for air. The sun gleaned in her eyes, but another wave grabbed her and pulled her under.

No!

She had to stay calm. She knew how to swim. Lauren hovered above the water again to see the boat was circling back.

"Hey!" she shouted. "Tom, stop!"

Lauren had no idea if they heard her. On the boat, she could see Amy doubling over with laughter, which made Lauren's blood burn. This wasn't funny. She could have been hurt.

Just as Lauren was swimming in the direction of the boat, she noticed something up ahead—something dark, floating in the water. Driftwood, maybe.

Frowning, Lauren got closer. It looked like somebody was in the water.

"Hey!" she shouted. "Are you okay? Do you need help?"

Her voice was whipped away by the wind and the boat's engine. Still, Lauren swam closer and closer.

The figure was tall, with long, dark hair that spread out behind it. It wasn't moving.

Lauren felt a chill run through her. It was then that she saw the person's face.

It was a face of horror. A face of pain.

It was a face of death.

A dead body.

Lauren screamed so loud, it grated against her throat.

CHAPTER TWO

Agent Lily Dawn stepped into her apartment in Quantico, Virginia, and sighed. The sun had just set through the white silk curtains that hung from the windows, and a soft glow filled her home. She took off her jacket and hung it on the coatrack, then padded into the kitchen to pour herself some wine.

Another case down. Another criminal put behind bars.

Lily's head was pounding. It'd been two weeks since she'd slept in her own bed, been in her own home. Lily poured herself a glass of the dark red wine and downed half of it. Sighing, she leaned against the counter and sipped her drink. The earthy, robust flavor took her away—but only for a moment.

This case had taken its toll on her, and she felt it in every heavy muscle on her body.

She'd been working the case for two full weeks—two full weeks of investigating and digging around in the underbelly of Washington DC's crime scene. Lily had gone undercover as a drug dealer, and she'd played the role well, even saving face when having to deal with all of the disgusting criminals who'd tried hitting on her. But Lily knew how to handle guys like them—a bit of charm, a bit of sexuality, but also a take-no-shit attitude would keep them interested in her enough to take her seriously.

The FBI had been fairly certain that one of the guys Lily had gotten close to, Geordie Stone, was a major player in a human trafficking ring that had been operating for at least five years.

They'd been right.

It was Lily who got close to him, who learned his tricks, and who finally took him down.

It was also Lily who got the brunt of his anger.

The actual takedown had been . . . messy. Lily was sure her neck was a little bruised from when Geordie had grabbed her roughly. Her wrists still stung from him manhandling her. Even her cheek was sore—when he'd realized he was caught, he'd given her a solid smack in the face, and she was certain that she'd be sporting some colorful bruises from it later on.

But still, she'd received praise from her boss earlier, and that had made it all feel worth it. Geordie Stone wouldn't harm any more girls. Lily had done her job.

Now, she had a moment to herself. She listened to the soft hum of her refrigerator before she went into her living room and sat down on the couch. Two weeks of stress melted her to the cushions.

At twenty-eight, Lily had been with the FBI for seven years, ever since she was fresh out of the academy. She couldn't imagine life being any other way. But damn, it was exhausting sometimes.

Lily sighed and glanced over at the table beside her couch. On it was a picture of Lily and her parents, taken over ten years ago, when Lily was only seventeen years old. In the photo, her parents and her were standing on the beaches of Aruba—the island she was born on—which was in the Caribbean but owned by the Netherlands. Lily's mom, Eline, was a Dutch-born philanthropist, and her father, Ramon, was from the Dominican Republic. Lily was a clear mix of both of them; she had her mom's blonde hair and blue eyes but her dad's tawny skin tone and full lips. Lily was proud of her appearance; she was proud of the way she carried on the genes of both her parents, who were great people. Her unique appearance had attracted some foul men in her time, though. Lily inwardly groaned just remembering Geordie, how he'd called her an "exotic beauty," and how she'd had to pretend to like it.

It was dehumanizing.

But Lily's job as a BAU agent wasn't to have emotions. It was to take down criminals. And that was what she'd done.

The sound of Lily's phone buzzing on the coffee table pulled her from her trance, and she swiped it up. The name on her screen made her stomach knot with dread.

Eduardo.

She hesitated before she answered.

"Ed, what—"

"Lily, just listen," he slurred.

She scowled, immediately put off. "You're drunk."

"I'm not. I just—" He stopped himself. The line went silent.

Lily knew Eduardo hadn't been doing well since their breakup. He'd sent texts and called a few times, but she'd made up her mind.

"Look, Ed," she said. "You know I can't give you what you want. My workload is insane. I'm too busy. And I'm not ready to settle down and start a family with you. That might be your future, but it's not mine."

Lily had dated Eduardo for a year, but it'd been too hard to have a relationship with a man who needed her to be present more than she could. Plus, he wanted kids. Lily had seen enough loss in her life to know that she wasn't ready for that level of responsibility. She'd watched her parents struggle, and Lily didn't want to put herself through a life like that.

"But you love me," he whined.

Lily leaned forward and pinched the bridge of her nose. "Yeah, I do."

"So, you'll marry me then."

Lily felt her blood run cold, but she managed to keep her voice steady. "No, Ed. I can't. You should move on."

"Don't be like that," Eduardo pleaded. "Don't throw us away."

"I can't."

"You love me, Lily. You can't tell me you don't."

"I do love you, but I'm not ready for this—"

"Bullshit! I'm not going to fucking sit around, waiting for you to come around and marry me, Lily. I can't wait forever."

Inside, Lily hardened. She scowled as she sat up straight, taking a sip from her wine glass.

"Then don't," she said and hung up, tossing the phone to the couch beside her. It buzzed again, but she ignored it.

Eduardo had been a sweet boyfriend, and in many ways, Lily did love him. She wished him nothing but the best. But she was on her own now, and Eduardo was free to find a girl who didn't work for the FBI and who didn't disappear for weeks, sometimes months, at a time.

He needed more than what she could give him. Maybe he didn't see it that way now, but Lily had set him free.

Lily picked up her glass of wine, swishing it around in her mouth before swallowing it whole. She was mostly a beer drinker, but she loved a good glass of wine every once in a while. She tipped it back again, and after a few moments, she felt the need to open up. She looked back at the picture of her parents.

"Mama, Papa," Lily said, sighing. "I miss you both." She drank again, hoping the alcohol would make her feel a little better, a little more at ease with herself. She lay back on the couch and closed her eyes, her mind drifting to better days—simpler days.

When she was alone, she often wondered what her parents were doing now. It had been so long since she'd spoken to them. She wondered if her dad still ran the restaurant. She wondered if her mom was still helping people. She didn't have the heart to search them online; it stirred up too many feelings, too many memories.

There was a reason they didn't talk anymore. Reasons that were too painful for Lily to think about.

Instead, she finished her wine, lulling herself into a state of peace.

Some days, alone on her couch with a glass of wine was the only peace she got.

In the morning, she'd be back to Quantico. Back to business.

*

Something crashed in Lily's apartment. Her eyes slowly fluttered open to her living room, and her brain raced to catch up with reality. Had that sound been real?

Another crash, somewhere in the kitchen.

Lily jolted up with a start on her living room coach, her heart pounding in her ears.

Someone's here.

Darkness blanketed the world outside. Her wall clock ticked. Loudly. Slowly. It almost didn't feel real.

Lily's wine glass was on the carpet, shattered. When had that happened?

Her heart felt like it was hammering at the walls of her throat, and she scrambled toward her table beside the couch. Her gun was in its holster, the bullets in their magazine, cooled and ready. She pulled it out of the holster, her hands trembling.

Lily held the gun, her hand on the trigger, and she closed her eyes for a moment, trying to quiet her nerves.

For a moment, she considered reaching for her phone and calling for backup. But there was no time. Someone was here.

Another crash in the kitchen. She heard the refrigerator door open, then slam shut. Glasses clinked.

A glint of light caught her eye. It came from the kitchen. A blade.

Her feet took her to the kitchen on their own. Her gun was raised, firmly grasped in her hands, but her arms shook. Lily inhaled a trembling breath as she stepped toward the doorway to her kitchen.

As the kitchen came into view, she could see that there was a person there, standing with their back facing her.

A woman. No—a girl with short, curly black hair.

A girl who had inherited their father's hair, not their mother's like Lily had.

Her heart stopped, but she didn't let go of the gun. *This isn't real*, she thought. *This can't be real.*

But there was Kara. Her sister. Her sister who went missing ten years ago was right there in Lily's kitchen.

"Kara?" Lily dared to ask.

Kara refused to turn around, but her body trembled. Lily's mouth was as dry as sand. She couldn't bring herself to move, to lower her gun. Instead, she stepped into the kitchen. The light flickered.

"Kara," Lily managed.

Slowly—finally—Kara turned around.

But Kara's familiar brown eyes weren't there.

They were black, empty pits, like her eyes had been carved out.

Lily staggered back. Her gun dropped from her hand, and she fell onto the floor as Kara towered over her.

"You left me," Kara said. "You left me!"

"No!" Lily rushed back on the heels of her palms. Kara's black, endless eyes bore into her until the walls around them started to shake. The plates in the shelves rattled and fell out, breaking all over the ceramic floor.

Lily screamed. She covered her ears with her palms. "No! No!"

Lily's eyes popped open to her dark, quiet living room. She was back on the couch. This time, her glass of wine was only half-finished—and still in her hand.

A dream? Her mind raced. It had felt so real.

Kara?

Lily tried to remember. Her heart was still pounding in her ears. It was like she was still there, in the dream, with Kara towering over her.

Kara . . .

"No," Lily said, shaking her head. It couldn't have been real. It had to have been a dream. A nightmare. Kara went missing ten years ago. Her body had never been found, but she'd been declared legally dead by authorities in the Caribbean—where they'd lived when she went missing—only a year ago.

It had been like losing her all over again. Lily had been able to talk to her parents on the phone then, but it had been brief. She knew that they still blamed her for Kara's disappearance.

More often than not, Lily blamed herself.

Lily's phone, still beside her on the couch, buzzed. She put her wine glass down. Through the windows, the sun was just rising, and the clock read five a.m. Still shaken up from the dream, Lily picked up her phone, half expecting it to be Eduardo, but it was her boss, Chief Sean Brock. Lily took a breath to collect herself before she answered.

"Chief Brock?"

"Agent Dawn," his familiar, brassy voice said. "Sorry to call so early. Did I wake you?"

Lily looked at the state of herself—still fully clothed, just sitting on her couch where she'd passed out. "No, of course not, Chief," she said. "What can I do for you?"

"Good." He paused for a moment. "I need you to get to HQ ASAP. It's important."

Lily's heart picked up. The chief wouldn't say it was important if it wasn't dire. "What's going on?"

"We'll talk when you get in." With that, the chief hung up, leaving Lily with her thoughts.

She sat there for a moment, processing his words.

An urgent call from the chief could only mean one thing:

She already had a new case.

And by the sound of his voice on that call, it was an important one.

CHAPTER THREE

Lily's shoes clacked on the floor as she made her way through the FBI headquarters in Quantico. Nerves pinched inside her chest. She had no idea what the chief wanted to have a meeting about, but she hoped that it would be a new, challenging case. As an agent of the BAU, Lily specialized in behavior analysis and did well undercover. However, she normally didn't stray far from Quantico, and she wouldn't mind a change of scenery.

Virginia was a good state. But the truth was, it wasn't home. Not to Lily.

Memories of her dream last night snuck into her mind as she rounded the corner, but she shook them away.

It wasn't real.

Kara's gone.

She arrived at Chief Brock's office and knocked, pushing the door open. The morning sun seeped through the window behind Chief Brock's desk, illuminating the plants in the room. Chief Brock was already behind his desk, his bald, dark-skinned head gleaming in the light.

But he wasn't alone.

Lily's heart stalled.

Director Brad Davy was sitting in one of the two chairs in front of the chief's desk. If Lily wasn't awake before, she was now.

It was rare to see Director Davy in person. He was a notoriously busy man, and his rank was even higher than Chief Brock's. If he was here, Lily could only assume one of two things:

One—she was in trouble for something.

Two—an extremely important case was about to be dropped on her lap.

"Agent Dawn, good morning," Director Davy said. He was a tall, narrow-faced man with gray hair, and he held himself with both poise and authority. Lily had always respected him from afar, but she'd rarely had the chance to talk to him face-to-face.

"Good morning, sir," Lily said, snapping to attention.

Director Davy gestured for her to sit down in the chair next to him.

Anxiety popped off in Lily's mind. What if I did something wrong in the Geordie Stone case? What if there's more to the story? Either way, Lily sat down and cleared her throat.

"First of all, I wanted to congratulate you on a job well done," Director Davy said.

Lily's eyes widened. "Sir?"

"Agent Dawn," Director Davy said. "You did a remarkable job on the Geordie Stone case. Your plan was bold and risky, but it was also the only way to get him. Remarkable job, really."

Heat rushed to Lily's cheeks, and she nodded. As much as she felt that she could've done a better job, sometimes it was more professional to just be humble and accept the praise. And she wasn't about to argue with a man like Director Davy. Maybe this meant she really wasn't in trouble.

"But," Chief Brock said, "that isn't all we called you in for."

Lily took a moment to take it all in. The two men were looking at her with grave expressions, and Lily's palms grew sweaty.

"We have a case for you, Agent Dawn," Director Davy said. "A unique case that I think might be perfect for you."

Lily's heart rate picked up. A momentary jolt of excitement went through her. "What kind of case?"

Chief Brock cleared his throat and said, "We're creating an experimental new task force. Homicide is on the rise at sea, in the gulf, and in the coastal areas of the Caribbean. Authorities feel that killers are exploiting the jurisdiction issues and using the cover of drugs."

The Caribbean. Nostalgia for a time long gone flowed through her. While Lily was born in Aruba, her dad was from the Dominican Republic, and Lily had spent years of her life there. They'd moved back and forth a few times, but after Kara's disappearance, her parents stayed in Aruba permanently.

Lily would always long for the islands. And now she was going back for work? It almost didn't feel real.

She snapped back to the conversation when Director Davy picked up where Chief Brock left off. He said, "A joint task force is being created between the FBI and the law enforcement of multiple Caribbean nations, most notably the Greater Antilles, to deal with homicide crime that has fallen into a jurisdictional gray area." Director

Davy's gray eyes met Lily's. "And Agent Dawn, we want you on this team for the first mission."

Lily blinked, processing the director's words. They wanted her to return home. To work in the Caribbean—where Kara went missing.

She found herself speechless. Lily was an experienced agent by now, and it was only a matter of time before her superiors started looking to give her bigger jobs and more responsibility. But now, faced with the task of returning home to the islands, Lily felt both nervousness and excitement rush through her veins.

Nervous because what if it stirred up old feelings? What if she became distracted or disoriented?

But excited because Lily had longed to return to the islands again. She'd gone to high school in Aruba and spent most of her life there.

It was also where she'd lost Kara.

When Lily didn't respond, Director Davy said, "You're the perfect person to help us get started out. You're young, you're bright, and you have an excellent track record."

"And you're from the islands," Chief Brock said. "You know the terrain."

Lily swallowed. She'd been in the FBI for only seven years, but she had the experience of a lifetime. And she did have the passion for this job. She thought about all the bodies she'd seen and all the families she'd helped.

She bit her lip. It would be crazy to pass this opportunity up, but she needed more details.

"Will I be fully relocating?"

"It's a temporary relocation," Chief Brock said. "We'll set you up with an apartment over there. And you won't be alone. You'll have a new partner, and the resources of the FBI behind you. Once the case is solved, you can return here, and we'll figure out our next steps."

"It's a big change," Director Davy added. "But we need to know your decision today, because we've just been notified that another body has been found."

Lily's stomach fell. "A body?"

The chief nodded. "Afraid so. A young heiress, a girl from a powerful family, was found dead in international waters near the Bahamas. We need to find out who killed her, and we need to do it fast—before another girl dies."

Lily's pulse quickened. This job was everything she'd ever wanted. The Caribbean, a new partner, and a real case that would change everything. After leaving Eduardo, Lily had been hoping for a clean slate. This case was the exact thing she needed to thrust her out of the stagnant life she'd been living in Quantico.

She wasn't going to let herself pass up something like this.

"Let's do it," Lily said.

"Excellent," Davy said, standing up. "Agent Dawn, welcome to the team."

Lily stood up and shook his hand, then Chief Brock's.

"And welcome back to the Caribbean," Chief Brock said.

"Thank you, sirs," Lily said. "I won't let the bureau down."

Director Davy smiled. "I know you won't, Agent Dawn."

Chief Brock handed Lily a file. "This has everything you need to know about the victims. Right now, authorities have no leads on who could be doing it. Although there is some speculation that the cartel could be involved, there's no evidence to back that claim up."

Lily opened the file and looked at the picture of the girl. She was twenty-two with long brown hair and a pretty, oval face. Marie Levesque. Looking at her photo made Lily's stomach churn; it was always difficult to see these girls alive and well, knowing they'd already lost their lives. Marie had been found floating in the water off the coast. The first victim, Sophia, had been found only days prior in a similar way—floating off the coast.

"We can't have another girl die," Chief Brock said. "I trust that you'll do everything in your power to make sure that doesn't happen."

Lily looked up and met Chief Brock's brown eyes. "I understand," she said. "I won't let this case go."

Lily felt a rush of excitement. She was going back to the islands. To the place where Kara disappeared. The place where she'd spent so many years of her life.

Lily's stomach churned with anxiety and excitement. Chief Brock was right about one thing—this was Lily's terrain. She knew the islands well.

Whoever was killing these girls needed to watch out. Because their reign of terror was about to end.

CHAPTER FOUR

Lily's breath caught as the shape of the Bahamas appeared over the horizon. The green land masses rolled out from beyond the window of her plane. The small islands that dotted the surrounding waters called to her like a song, and she longed to visit each one, to see what might be hidden in their crevices, caves, and jungles.

The FBI had expedited her on a private jet to get her there ASAP. Not even three hours ago, she'd packed up everything she needed from her apartment for the trip, as it was undetermined how long she'd be staying in the Bahamas. Lily was certainly in no rush to get back to the US. Ideally, they would find this criminal quickly and put him behind bars—but after that, Lily hoped her relocation to the Bahamas might become more permanent. It had been a long time since she'd felt so excited, so eager to get to work.

Turning away from the window, she refocused on the case files, which she had open on her lap.

Several young women had been killed in Freeport in recent years, but the two latest were notable because they were both found floating aimlessly in the ocean, like their bodies had been dumped without a care. Lily's stomach twisted at the idea. There was something so sinister about just leaving them, not even bothering to conceal the evidence, burn the bodies, or do anything to hide the crime other than dump the girls like garbage into the sea.

They deserved a better ending than that.

Lily could never bring their lives back, she knew that. But she could give them justice by taking down who hurt them. It was the best thing—the only thing—she could do.

The first victim had been Sophia Harris, a rich girl from Utah who had been vacationing in Freeport alone. The file noted that Sophia had a large social media following, and she'd gone on the solo trip as something to share with her followers. It was worth noting, in Lily's eyes, that Sophia had been very public with her whereabouts online, which could have attracted a stalker.

That wouldn't explain why Marie Levesque—the most recent victim—was found dead in the same way, though.

Marie was a French-born American citizen and heiress to a massive fortune. She was also travelling alone. However, Marie's social media presence was very modest in comparison to Sophia's. Lily had no reason to believe, on a surface level, that Sophia could have had a stalker who also noticed Marie online.

But there could be a stalker who saw them both on the island.

After all, they were both travelling alone.

Lily looked at the photos of each victim from when they were alive. They were both brunettes in their twenties, smiling. Beautiful, with an air of wealth. But their appearances were quite different, aside from the hair: Marie was pale-skinned. Sophia had a sandier complexion. Plus, their facial features were vastly different.

Lily looked closer.

Marie had a birthmark on her arm in one of the photos. It was a large, dark splotch over her forearm.

She looked closer at the photo of Sophia, who was standing on a beach in a white dress. It was hard to say if Sophia had a similar mark. But she had only died a few days ago.

Lily swallowed hard. It might be a coincidence, but something told her there was something even more sinister at play.

Either way, arriving at the island would hopefully bring her more answers. She closed the file and watched as the plane descended toward the island. She wondered who her new partner would be and hoped it would be someone she liked, but she knew that wasn't always the case for FBI agents starting out on a new team. There was always a honeymoon period, a sort of settling-in time. She would get through it, and she was excited to use her experience to help her new partner.

Lily felt like she was a part of something big. She didn't know exactly what it was yet, but she felt it deep in her bones. Her fingers twitched with anticipation. She'd always wanted to return to the islands. And now that she had the chance, she wouldn't let it slip away.

She couldn't.

Maybe once she was done with the job, she could even get some answers about Kara.

As the plane descended, Lily tried to shake off her nerves. She wasn't sure how the foreign agents and the locals were going to react to her—an FBI agent who had authority on their turf. She hoped that she'd be accepted, and she hoped that she would be an asset to them. Lily didn't feel like a foreigner here, but she knew some would view her that way.

She pushed the thoughts away and looked down at the sea, where the bays, inlets, and islands were spread out before her. The water was turquoise and calm, despite the growing tides inside Lily. Tides of uncertainty, of anxiety. She'd always considered herself good at keeping a cool exterior, but inside, Lily had her own doubts.

The plane touched down on the small runway. They had arrived in Freeport on the Grand Bahama Island. The Caribbean was hers.

Once the plane was fully stopped, Lily was instructed by the pilot that it was safe to leave. Lily grabbed her suitcase and left the plane. As soon as she exited, she felt the Bahamas sun on her face and breathed in the dense, humid, and salty air. It was a feeling she'd longed for so many times since moving to the US.

This isn't a vacation, she reminded herself. She couldn't enjoy it too much when there were girls in danger here—and girls who deserved justice.

Lily made her way down the stairs and got off on the landing strip, where there was a car waiting for her—and two men.

One of them was clearly the driver—a dark-skinned man who leaned against the hood of the car.

The other guy was . . . something else.

Tall and lean, he was wearing a pair of aviators that reflected the sun. As soon as he saw Lily with her suitcase, he strode right up to her like a male model on a runway. His skin was tanned from the sun, and he had short, highlighted blond hair. He took off his glasses to reveal eyes greener than algae at sea.

Lily instantly felt like this guy was something else. Trouble, most likely.

He held out a hand to her as they met. "Agent Dawn?"

Lily nodded. "Yes," she said, extending her hand.

He shook it firmly. *A military boy?* she wondered. "Agent Xander Jackson. Pleasure to make your acquaintance." He had a distinctly Southern accent—maybe Texas or Tennessee.

"Agent Lily Dawn," Lily said, shaking his hand back. Their eyes remained locked for a moment before he dropped his hand. Xander looked over his shoulder and nodded at the driver, beckoning him to come over. He took Lily's bag from her, but she resisted.

"Oh, that's okay," she said. "I can carry it myself."

"Ma'am, let me put this away for you," he said.

Xander gave Lily a look. "Let the man do his job."

Lily couldn't help but feel annoyed. Xander had a haughty attitude about him. But it wasn't worth arguing. She allowed the driver to take her bag and slot it into the trunk of the car.

Xander held the door open for Lily, and she got inside. At least he had manners. Although with her, manners weren't necessary.

She settled into the back of the car and buckled her seat belt. Xander got in the back beside her. Once the driver was behind the wheel, the car took off, and Lily knew there was no turning back now.

She was in this.

Beside her, Xander shot her a look as they drove. "They didn't tell me I was gettin' paired up with someone so young," he said.

Lily shot him a look. Young? Sure, but she was qualified. "I'm twenty-eight," Lily stated.

"Yeah, that's young, sweetheart," said Xander. "Talk to me once you've hit thirty."

Lily nearly rolled her eyes. If he thought he could give her attitude without getting it back, he was in for another story. "With that clean-shaven face of yours, I could mistake you for a kid too," she shot back.

He laughed and stroked his chin. "Never could grow a full beard. S'all right, though. I'll be thirty-five this fall." He clacked his tongue and shot her a wink. "Anyway, just follow my lead, all right? You'll be fine."

Lily scowled. She was used to dealing with arrogant men, but this guy was getting under her skin. "We're partners, Agent Jackson," she reminded him. "You're not my superior. We follow each other's leads."

That had him cackling. "Whatever you say, girly."

She couldn't believe that this was her new partner. They had one thing in common—they were with the FBI. Beyond that, he was a walking, talking stereotype, and Lily didn't know anything about who he was or where he came from. It seemed like he didn't know much about her, either.

Whatever, Lily thought. *This was just a temporary thing.* She'd had three different partners since her first partner, Special Agent Foster—who had been her treasured mentor—retired. Xander Jackson wouldn't last either.

"So," Xander said. He was wearing a Rolex on his wrist, and the sleeves of his white shirt were rolled up. "Let me just fill you in real quick on what we're dealing with here. Young woman, Marie Levesque, dead. Heiress to a huge fortune, born in France, but lived in the US of A. She was vacationing here alone when a couple found her dead, floating between the waters of the Bahamian Coast and mainland Florida. As of right now, we have no idea what happened to her."

"I read the files," Lily said. "Is there still no official cause of death?" Lily asked, building an image of this woman in her head. Cases like this always struck close to home. She worried that Marie's fate was the same as Kara's—although Kara's body had never been found.

"They've got her at the coroner's now, figuring it out," Xander replied.

"Then we should visit there first," Lily said.

"Absolutely," Xander agreed. "But first thing's first: we drop off our bags at our new place and get a car so Jorge here can keep working."

In the front, the driver stayed quiet. But one thing stood out that Xander said, one thing that made her stomach drop:

"Our?"

*

Lily stared into the open door of the house—which looked more like a luxury vacation rental than anything else: white beachy walls, an open concept design. She heard the distant waves hitting the shore.

"Home sweet home, sweetheart," Xander said, dropping his suitcase on the wooden floor.

If Lily had known that she'd be sharing a place with her new partner, she might have been less keen on coming. She stiffly held her suitcase in her hand, not wanting to let it drop—not wanting to accept her fate.

Beside her, Xander laughed. "Relax, Dawn. I'm told there's an entire suite upstairs, private bathroom and everything. All you've gotta do is share a kitchen with me." He strode into the house, then shot her a wink. "Can you handle that?"

Lily pushed past him, dragging her suitcase, and went toward the winding staircase. It didn't matter where she was staying as long as they were able to work on finding out what happened to those girls, and get it done fast, that was all that mattered. The house was small and narrow but gorgeous. "Let's just drop off our stuff and focus on the case," Lily said, hauling her suitcase upstairs. It felt more like a loft than an upper level of a house, but there was something charming about it, Lily had to admit. The sand dollars and starfish decorating the house reminded her of the home she'd had in Aruba, back when she and her family were on good terms, back when Lily still had a sister.

There was only one room upstairs, and Lily went inside. It was open and bright, with sandstone wallpaper and simple, bright, and beachy decal. A door led to her private bathroom, and she was grateful she wouldn't have to share too much of her space with Xander. This was private enough.

Lily left her suitcase to unpack later and went back downstairs. There was another room down there beside the small living room, presumably Xander's room. He came out of it and stretched his long arms, his aviators positioned on top of his head. "You all ripe and ready to go?"

Lily bit her tongue. She was going to have to get used to the way Xander talked, as much as it annoyed her. "Ready when you are," she said.

"Good." Xander stuck his hands in the pockets of his slacks. "Let's go get the rental car and see a dead body."

CHAPTER FIVE

Lily took in the scenery of Freeport, Bahamas, as Xander drove them in the rental car toward the coroner's office. The islands were picturesque—as picturesque as Lily remembered them. There wasn't a cloud in the bright blue skies above. She took in the view of the homes that lined the coast and smiled at some of the pastel-colored houses tucked into a hillside. They must have been built to withstand hurricanes, because every single house was exactly the same distance from the tree line. There were expensive beachfront homes and less expensive homes that sat higher on the coast, but they were all built to withstand storms or flooding.

It was so different from back in DC. Everything was so bright and cheerful in the Bahamas, which was a stark contrast to the cold, dreary DC—a stark contrast to the harshness of the real world. Being in a place like this could often feel like stepping out of reality and into paradise, but Lily knew there was still evil here; she could taste it on her tongue.

When she was younger, there were many times when Lily and her family had come to the Bahamas from Aruba to visit. It had been so many years, but Lily could easily remember roaming the sunny streets with Kara when they were girls: holding each other's hands as they ran through the streets, chasing wild cats and stopping to marvel at the beauty of some of the American tourists.

Not all the memories were good, though. There was one time, when Lily was nine and Kara was eight, that they were here—in Freeport—on vacation with their parents. They'd slipped away from the cottage to go see if they could buy some burnt almond cupcakes from the bakery without their parents knowing. Their dad didn't like them having sugar too early—it made them hyper all day, but Lily couldn't resist. The burnt almond cupcakes were something Lily had only ever seen here in Freeport, and Kara loved them. She had some change her dad had given her as an allowance, so she wanted to treat them.

But as Lily and Kara were making their way through the streets—they cut through an alleyway to get there faster—they'd heard a man's voice.

Up the alleyway, a tall and broad-shouldered man covered in tribal tattoos was holding another man against the wall by his throat. A knife was on the ground, unsheathed.

The tall man had a hand to the other man's throat and his forearm against his neck so that he could control him, and he was shaking him by his collar. The other man's face was turning red from straining so hard to speak.

"P . . . please, man! I'll pay you! I promise!"

Lily and Kara didn't know what they were seeing, but Lily's instincts activated.

They had to get away.

Scurrying down the alleyway, they attempted to hide behind a dumpster beside the building, but they could still hear the muffled sound of the beating, and the sound of the other man begging for his life.

They could save him, Lily had thought at the time. But what could two little girls do against a bad man? It felt like fate that they were brought to the scene and could see it from a distance. They could see their own possible future, in a way: one that ended in tragedy for them, or for the helpless man.

Lily was torn. Looking back on it, it was a huge burden for a nine-year-old. If she told their parents what they saw, they'd surely get in trouble for snooping around. If she left . . . maybe the man would get seriously hurt.

The fear had taken over, and Lily grabbed Kara's hand and ran her all the way back to the cottage, where the two girls slipped onto the property. Lily made Kara promise never to tell their parents what they saw.

As an adult, Lily realized that it was likely cartel related: a drug deal gone wrong, or a man who owed money and was refusing to pay up.

It was a dark memory, one she didn't like to think of too often. Lily was only a child, but she wasn't proud of herself for running away.

It was part of what fueled her to never run away again.

Even if the man being assaulted was a criminal, too, Lily didn't stand for needless violence. So, whoever had killed the two girls here on the island had a hellfire coming for them.

Lily was so lost in her memories, she almost forgot she was still driving with Xander. His voice, with his Southern drawl, broke her reverie.

"So, Agent Dawn," Xander began, glancing at her as he drove through a green light. His aviators reflected the afternoon sun. "What do you think about all this? We've got a string of murders, and this Marie chickie is just one of them. Seems like a pretty open-and-shut cartel case if you ask me. Lots of crime around here dealing with that."

Lily shot him a frown. "That's all you think it is?"

He shrugged. "Think about it. Rich, beautiful girl here vacationing all alone. Bound to get noticed by some seedy characters if she's not careful. I think she attracted the wrong guy, and he did her one. She's the second rich girl for this to happen to in the past few days, so something tells me the cartel is robbing beauties."

Lily considered his words. It wouldn't be the first time the cartel has gotten involved with tourists—but it seemed too easy. Lily wasn't willing to pass it off just yet—she needed to know more.

"I doubt it's so simple," Lily said. She pulled out the case file, which was on the floor of the car, and opened it up, reviewing it carefully.

"You got a scent on this one, then?" Xander asked.

"No," Lily admitted. "The police haven't really found anything useful. But that's why the FBI's here."

"Touché, sweetheart."

Lily couldn't resist her annoyance. "Can you stop with the 'sweetheart' shit? It's getting old fast."

"Oh, come on," he said, turning his eyes back to the road. "Have a little fun. This is the Bahamas, after all. You don't have to be a stick in the mud twenty-four-seven, darling."

Lily couldn't believe this guy. What was the FBI thinking by pairing her up with him? Why was he even an agent? Lily hoped that he was at least brave and capable under this layer of annoyance, but she was having a hard time picturing a clean future with this guy as her partner.

"This is the job, and I'm not going to have any fun until we find the killer," she said.

"If it's more than cartel, it could be a hard nut to crack," he said, drumming his fingers on the steering wheel. "We're in a whole new territory here. I've been to Freeport before, I know how beautiful it is here. But there are some pretty ugly things about this place as well. When you've lived as long as I have, you get to see it all. The good, the bad, and the ugly."

"You're thirty-five, not sixty, Agent Jackson," Lily muttered.

But Xander just laughed. "I've seen a lot in my day, though. Been in the Navy and the DEA." He shot her a look. "And what have you done?"

His eyes on her made her hair stand on end. "I've been with the FBI officially for seven years," she told him. "It's not a competition."

"Never said it was," he droned on. "I'm just trying to get to know my new partner." He shot her a wink. "Now I know you've never done anything but FBI, which you probably wouldn't have told me otherwise."

Lily bit back her response. It wasn't worth it, and this banter was a waste of time. She had a crime to solve, so she refocused on the case files.

"Is Sophia Harris's body still at the coroner's?" Lily asked.

"Sure is," Xander said. "They were set to expedite her, but once the second body dropped, they kept her until we got there so we could see if there's a connection."

Lily nodded. As much as Xander was rubbing her the wrong way, she was a professional, and she could handle him. It was better to keep trying to get along. "Good thinking."

"Now, I'm not saying there's a connection," Xander said. "But you've got to check these things out. My gut is the cartel did this, like they've been doing for years. My instincts have never steered me wrong."

Lily nodded, sinking in her seat. She didn't know what she was expecting to find at the coroner's. But she knew that there were two women who were found dead in similar ways. She knew that there was something deeper going on.

If it was the cartel, then so be it. But Lily was here to uncover the truth, not blindly follow a gut instinct.

The car pulled up outside of a small, sterile building that was the coroner's office. Palm trees grew on the lawn, and there were only a couple of cars in the parking lot. Xander pulled in and gave her a look. "Well, Agent Dawn, we're here. Ready to see some dead bodies?"

Lily's eyes hardened on the building, nervous for what she was about to see in there. "Ready as I'll ever be. Let's go."

CHAPTER SIX

Xander didn't like the look on his new partner's face. He hadn't figured Lily Dawn out yet, but he wasn't stupid. Something was bothering the girl. All he had to do was wait until she got more comfortable with him, and then he'd have her story.

It wasn't his experience—or his habit—to force people to talk. He always let the people around him open up on their own. It was something he learned from the Navy SEALs, and it always worked. People would talk on their own if you gave them enough space. His tactic was to prod a little and ask a few questions here and there to get the gears in their heads turning. In some cases, Xander could play up a person's emotions to get them to reveal something they didn't necessarily wish to reveal—such as earlier when he'd gotten Lily to admit how long she'd been in the FBI. Seven years. It wasn't bad, he had to admit, and this girl was a bit of a firecracker. But he was a bit leery of how young she was.

Just gives you a reason to be in charge, he reminded himself. And he had to admit, she was easy on the eyes: blue irises, blonde hair, curvy body, and a nice, deep tan. He'd never seen someone who looked quite like her, and he tried not to let it distract him.

After getting out of the car, Xander and Lily made their way toward the coroner's building. He could tell she was nervous to see the bodies. Two pretty, young girls found dead and bloated—it was going to be a grisly sight. But Xander had killed plenty of badasses in his days, and he wasn't afraid of a little dead body.

"Let's get this over with," Lily said when they walked in the door.

Xander shrugged, heading down the hall with her. There were signs and posters to steer the visitors in the direction they needed to go, just like in any hospital. As they walked, Lily scanned the brightly lit and well-maintained halls with a look of distraction, and Xander couldn't help but wonder what was going through her head right now. Nervousness? Anxiety? Frustration?

The coroner's office was just like any other they'd seen—immaculately clean, with a stainless-steel counter that gleamed under the fluorescent lights. He waited as Lily signed her name in a little logbook, then headed to the receptionist's desk.

"Agent Dawn and Agent Jackson here to see the coroner," Lily said before Xander even had the chance to speak up. He raised his eyebrows and backed off. He could tell this girl was going to try to run the show, but that wouldn't get her far with him.

Xander was older, more experienced. Even if they were equals on a status level in the FBI, Xander was gunning for a promotion to special agent. This case, he figured, would be his golden ticket. He needed to lead it, to take home the gold and find out what this was all about.

"Right this way," the receptionist said, gesturing to a room. Xander and Lily followed.

They were led into a sterile, white room that smelled of antiseptic and formaldehyde. There were two large metal tables, where two corpses were covered with white sheets. The room felt warmer than it ought to, and Xander wondered if the air-conditioning was on the fritz. A man with a mask on sat up from a computer that was in the corner of the room.

"You must be the two agents," he said.

"We are," Lily replied. "I see you got the girls out already."

"Yes, this is them," he said.

"Mind if I take a look?" Lily asked.

"Go right ahead," the coroner said. "We're still gathering forensic data on them, and I haven't performed an official autopsy on the latest victim."

Lily nodded, pulling on a set of thin, blue-paper gloves. She slipped her hand under the sheet covering the first woman, pulling it back gingerly. She blinked at the sight of it, then looked up at Xander.

Xander peered down at the bodies, his stoic mask firmly in place.

Even he had to admit that it wasn't a pretty sight.

Sophia Harris, the rich girl from Utah, was dead, bloated, pale, waterlogged . . . you name it.

Marie Levesque, the heiress from France, was in just as bad shape—but she had a bit more color than Sophia, considering she'd likely been killed after her. Xander had half a mind to slap on some gloves himself and take control, but he decided to take a back seat for just a bit—see how Agent Lily Dawn could handle the pressure of looking at a dead body up close.

He could tell it was bothering her, the sight of all that bloated, dead flesh. Xander felt sorry for her and thought he'd give her a break.

"Can you check to see if they share any identifying features?" Xander asked the coroner.

"I can try," he replied. "I didn't even get a chance to run the forensic computer yet. I can't promise you anything. Probably just height and weight unless we find a tattoo or a distinctive birthmark."

"It'll do, for now."

The coroner nodded, touching the computer, typing in *Sophia Harris*. "Height five foot, six inches. Weight, 140 pounds."

Lily was wincing, taking this in, but she wasn't turning around. Xander had to give her props for sticking it out. Maybe she was stronger than he was giving her credit for.

"What about the next one?" she asked.

The coroner let out a little sigh and tapped his computer again. "Marie Levesque was five foot, six inches. Weight, 136 pounds."

Lily nodded, biting her lip. "I . . . see."

She traced Sophia's neck, feeling around the bloated skin. She looked back up at the coroner.

"There's a bit of a ligature mark here," Lily said. "Nothing too deep, but it's possible there was rope here at some point before she died."

"Mm, good eye," the coroner agreed. "It's pretty hard to tell with all the, well, bloated flesh. We are still not entirely sure what killed these girls; it appears to be drowning, but we're waiting for toxicology reports. Something could still come up."

Lily nodded, standing back. "Make sure you call us right away when you have confirmation." Then, she looked at Xander. "They were both tourists, both travelling alone, both from wealthy backgrounds . . ."

"Yeah, almost like they were prime bait for the cartel," Xander said. He still felt like that was the most likely option here. Two pretty, rich things on their own could easily attract the wrong types of guys, and even the bees on this island knew that the cartel presence was strong.

It was a risk, though, for them to murder two rich tourists. Xander had to admit that put a bit of a hole in his theory. If—when—this got out, it would deter Americans from coming, which would cut off a huge portion of the cartel's drug sales. Rich Americans loved coming to an island paradise to party and blow their cash. They didn't come to get murdered.

"I'm still not sold on the cartel theory," Lily said. She reached into her side pack and pulled out a file, flipping it open and reading it. "Sophia Harris, Victim One, wasn't just a rich girl with a big social media following; her dad is the governor of Utah. And Marie, Victim Two, was an heiress; her father was also a rich and powerful man."

"So, what," Xander said. "You think this has something to do with daddy issues?"

She shot him a sour look. Probably not liking his attitude, but Xander didn't care about that. He knew he wasn't every woman's cup of tea, and Lily was handling him better than a lot of his previous partners had. But there was a reason Xander had such a long and successful career. He got results.

"I don't know what it is yet," Lily said. "But I think we should start from the beginning. I think we should focus on Sophia—she was the first victim, after all."

Xander thought on it. "But Marie Levesque is the VIP. We should focus on her first."

Lily glowered slightly, like she didn't like Xander talking back to her. *Get used to it, sweetheart,* he thought, but kept himself together because the coroner was still in the room.

"I think we should focus on Marie," Xander added on. "Start with the fresh meat, then dial it back."

"Agent Jackson, please do not call them 'fresh meat,'" Lily said, her voice firm, but he could tell she was getting pissed at him. *Maybe I should dial it back,* he thought.

Xander raised his hands. "Sorry. My point is, Marie is our latest victim and I think we have a higher likelihood of sniffing out her trail."

"But Sophia was the first," she countered.

Xander rolled his eyes. "Yes, of course she was the first. But it's hard to go looking for the first."

"I'm not sure that makes any more sense."

Tough shit, he thought, giving her a cool look. *If she doesn't like it, she can work her way up to my level to be able to talk to me like that.* In all his years, he didn't think anyone had ever been able to tell him what to do when it came to leading a case. "Look, Agent Dawn, we are not on an equal footing here. I am, frankly, your superior, and I will lead this case in the way that I see fit. I understand that you're new to the field, but I'm experienced, and I get results, so I'm going to make all the decisions."

Lily bristled, her jaw tightening. He could see anger flash through her eyes, and for a moment, he almost regretted it.

"We are equals, Agent Jackson," Lily uttered, her tanned cheeks flushing. "Call yourself my superior one more time and I'll be getting Director Davy on the line. I was not sent here to be your subordinate—I was sent here to be your partner, and you're crossing a line with the way you're talking to me."

Shit. She had him there. Davy would definitely give Xander shit for pissing off his new partner.

I need to behave a bit more, he reminded himself, but it was hard to keep himself in check. It was just his personality.

But Lily was no wet blanket. In fact, this girl had spark. Xander had to respect it—she'd put him in his place.

So, he cracked a smile.

"All right, all right," he said. "I'm messing with you, sort of. Have it your way, Agent Dawn. We'll look into Sophia Harris first."

Lily was taking a deep breath, a little annoyed, but Xander didn't need to push her too hard to get her to agree. When she saw her opening, she took it, and that was okay by him.

"Thank you," she said. "And I know exactly where we should start."

"Oh, yeah?" Xander said.

Lily nodded. "The hotel where Sophia was staying."

Xander nodded. He'd started to think the same exact thing. He smiled a little to himself. She might be hot stuff, but her thinking like a detective was a bit more than he'd thought.

He'd have to step up his game.

CHAPTER SEVEN

Lily needed to keep her emotions in check as Xander drove them toward the hotel, navigating the streets of Freeport. He really was testing her patience, but she had to stay professional—she had to handle him.

Maybe dealing with a guy like him was a test from the FBI. A test to see how well Lily could handle pressure. How well she could work with people, even when they made her want to claw her eyes out.

Even during the case itself, she'd noticed how Xander had grown more and more impatient. She'd seen how he talked back, which was something Lily had just started to let slide. It was hard to stand her ground against an experienced agent like him and not let the ego trip get to her, but she had to do it by the book.

Maybe that's why they put me with him, she thought. *They knew I could handle him.*

So far, she'd passed though, which made her proud. She was handling this asshole. She was using him to her advantage, and she was getting a chance to show what she could do.

As he turned the corner, heading south on the main road that led away from the airport, she reached over and turned off the radio, cutting out the only noise in the car. She stared out the window, thinking.

She couldn't deny that he was gorgeous. That was obvious, and between that and the way the shape of his muscular body looked, it was hard to not to let her mind drift off in fantasies involving him getting naked.

But he was a Class A jerk, mostly. He was used to calling the shots, used to being in control, and used to people not arguing with him about how to do his job. That was probably why he was an agent—for all his flakiness, trouble, and asshole behavior, he still got results. He was a box office hit when it came to investigating things.

But as they headed toward the hotel where Sophia had been staying, she had to admit that if working with Xander and putting up with his haughtiness would help her find out what happened to those girls, then so be it.

The hotel itself was a quaint little place on the north end of Freeport—a small boutique hotel tucked into the city center, just a few blocks away from the main tourist destination, Trade Island. Right at the heart of it, where the hotel was located, was the heart of the city.

That was what Lily liked about it—it brought the old and the new together, blending different kinds of people and different kinds of lifestyles, bringing them all into one place. Sophia must have thought this would be the perfect vacation destination to share with her social media followers.

Xander turned off the engine once he found a parking spot. Lily wasn't sure what she'd find here, but she figured talking to the staff inside would be the best bet. She unbuckled her seatbelt and got out of the car, feeling the hot sun on her skin.

It was nice to get out of the stuffy vehicle for a bit.

Xander got out as well, shoving his hands in the pockets of his pants. He glanced over at Lily, raising an eyebrow.

"Ready to start another adventure, Ms. Dawn?"

Lily resisted rolling her eyes. "That's Agent Dawn, Agent Jackson," she shot back.

He smirked. "Yes, ma'am," he said, showing her to the front door of the hotel.

"Oh, we are so starting this all over again," she muttered to herself, but didn't say anything directly to him. *Keep your temper in check,* she reminded herself. Although she was only human. She wondered how many times she'd have to handle Xander before she finally snapped.

She walked into the small reception area behind Xander. The place was pretty nice, she had to admit, with the beige walls and dark furniture giving the place a very chic atmosphere. The receptionist was a beautiful young woman sitting behind the front desk, smiling up at them sweetly. "May I help you guys?" she asked, looking from Xander to Lily.

Lily showed her badge, and so did Xander. "We're with the FBI," Lily said. "We were hoping to talk to you about one of your patrons, Sophia Harris."

The girl's face went pale. "You mean the girl who . . ."

"She was found dead, yeah," Xander cut in before Lily could. "We're trying to figure out what happened to her, so maybe you can start with what you saw of her when she was here."

She nodded. "Yes, of course. I had no idea that happened. That's so sad. She was such a lovely girl, honestly."

Lily and Xander leaned against the counter while the receptionist gathered her thoughts.

"Well, Sophia booked this room on the night she arrived, and she stayed here for the next three nights. She checked out on the morning of the fourth day."

"And what date was that, exactly?" Lily asked.

"Let me check . . ." The receptionist's fingers clacked against the keyboard as she typed into the computer. "It was July 7th."

"She was found dead later that day," Lily said, thinking out loud. "She checked out the same morning."

It could mean nothing—or it could be a clue. Lily wasn't sure yet.

"She checked out in person?" Xander asked. "Just out of bed and gone, no goodbyes or anything like that?"

The receptionist shook her head. "No, I checked her out for her. She was in and out of the room a lot during her stay, so all I had to do was get her signature on the withdrawal form and I was done."

"And did she give any indication as to where she was going after that?" Lily cut in.

"Not at all, I'm afraid," the receptionist said.

"And did you ever see Sophia with anyone?" Lily asked. "Did she have any boyfriends or friends, at the hotel?"

"Not that I ever saw," the receptionist said. "But I'm here all day. Our manager, Jorge, might be able to tell you more. He tends to keep an eye on the grounds."

"I'd like to speak to him, please," Lily said.

The receptionist picked up the phone and dialed a number. Lily got out of the way as the receptionist began to talk to someone on the other side of the line, telling him that the FBI would like to see him.

"All right, you can go back to the office," she said, ending the call. "Jorge is waiting for you there."

Lily nodded to the receptionist and then turned to Xander. "Let's see what he has to say," she said, following him to a door in the back of the reception area.

It opened into a small office, where there was a balding man sitting in front of a desk, looking over papers. He stood up when he saw them, his eyes wide and his hands trembling. He looked like a mouse about to be gobbled up by a cat.

"How can I help you, agents?" he asked, in a voice that cracked halfway through.

Lily took out her badge again and handed it to him. He took it in his hands and stared at the words, then looked back at the agents.

"We're on a case," Lily said, leaning forward. The man had a faint pheromone scent around him, a bit like cologne but sweeter. It made her slightly queasy. "We're trying to figure out what happened to a guest that was here, Sophia Harris. Maybe you've heard the news."

"I did," Jorge said, "and I've been wondering when someone would come to speak to us. I remember the Sophia Harris girl—she was hard to miss. A young, beautiful woman, she was. I saw her by the pool, mostly, and she was always on her phone."

"Did you ever see her with anyone?" Lily asked.

"Maybe a boyfriend," Xander added. "Or a guy who took a bit too much of a liking to her."

Jorge averted his eyes. "Oh, no. Not that I saw."

Lily squinted. Jorge rubbed the back of his neck and couldn't make eye contact. Was it just her, or was he hiding something?

"Please," Lily said. "If you saw anyone, anyone at all, talking to Sophia, please let us know. We are afraid this person could be a danger to other women on the island."

Jorge was quiet. Lily got the sense that it wasn't easy for him to trust law enforcement. She understood that; the Bahamas had a different society than the US, different level of trust of the government. But she needed to convince Jorge to speak up.

"Or any other part of the island," she added. "This person could be anywhere, and it's our job to track them down."

Jorge sighed, glancing up at her. "I'm not sure what to tell you," he said. "The only person I saw her talk to was a man who arrived in the middle of the night—I live at the hotel, so I tend to see everything that happens here. She went out to the beach with him, and they seemed to have a heated conversation. I could hear her yelling over the sounds of the ocean."

"Did he seem angry?" Lily asked.

"Definitely," Jorge said. "I was about to ask him who he was and what the fight was about when he stormed down the beach, and Sophia grabbed her things and went back to the hotel."

"Did you recognize this man at all?" Lily asked, her heart pounding. This could be huge. Whoever this guy was—if he was bothering Sophia, and then killed her . . . maybe that activated his thirst to kill again. To kill Marie.

And maybe he wouldn't stop there.

"I didn't, at first, but then he came back the next day," Jorge said. "He tried to find Sophia, but we refused to tell him where her room was. I have seen this man before—his name is Jose Alvarez, and if I remember right, he spends a lot of time at this real seedy club here on the island."

Lily exchanged a look with Xander, who nodded. This was a lead.

"We're gonna need the name of that club," Xander said.

"Okay," Jorge said. "It's called Club Rammer Jammer. The club's owner, a man named Charles Langle, will know who hangs out there, I'm sure."

Lily smiled grimly. "We're gonna need to go check it out," she said. "We'll be in touch."

"All right," Jorge said, his voice small and meek. "Good luck."

Xander and Lily nodded and turned to exit the office. Once in the hallway, heading out of the hotel, Lily pursed her lips.

"Expecting trouble?" Xander asked.

"Maybe," she said. She had a bad feeling about this one. This Alvarez guy could turn out to be trouble and going into a seedy club to find him could turn sideways fast.

But there was only one way to find out.

CHAPTER EIGHT

The outside of Club Rammer Jammer looked as seedy to Lily as it sounded.

The neon signs pulsed in the windows, colors shifting from green to red and back again. As Xander parked the car, that bad feeling continued to roil through Lily.

She only hoped that coming here wouldn't be a waste of time. She needed to find out how this Alvarez guy knew Sophia.

And if he was the killer.

"You ready to do this?" Xander asked, peering over at her as she opened the car door.

Lily said nothing. Of course, she was ready.

The inside of the club was tiny, a tight fit for even the dozen or so people scattered around the space. It was dimly lit, and there was an almost tangible mix of perfumes, colognes, and body odor in the air. From what Lily could see, the club was mostly filled with men.

A burly bouncer stepped up when they passed through the lobby. "ID?" he asked them.

"Well, isn't that sweet," Xander said, holding up his FBI badge. Lily did the same.

The bouncer's eyes narrowed. Maybe part of him felt like he should keep them out, but he decided against it, because he moved out of the way and let them past. A good move. Lily was sure that he didn't get paid enough to risk getting in trouble with the law.

Xander and Lily walked around the space, gazing at the men. The scene was reminiscent of US bars, Lily had to admit—the same overworked men looking for a good time.

There was something sad about that, she thought.

As they made their way to the bar, Lily took note of the looks they were getting. Unfriendly glances. Two men even chuckled to themselves, to which Lily noticed Xander's nostrils twitch.

"The fuck they laughing at?" he asked absentmindedly.

"Just focus on the case, Jackson," Lily said. She didn't feel like getting to know Xander's loose cannon side.

She wasn't even sure if she knew his sane side yet. So, she had to tip-toe a bit, at least until she got a better sense of him.

She just wanted this killer behind bars.

Xander gave her a look, but he kept quiet. As he slid onto one of the stools at the bar, Lily sat next to him. A bartender walked over to them, raising his eyes suspiciously. "What can I get you, guys?"

"Two tequila shots," Lily said, shooting Xander a look.

Xander returned it but didn't make another comment. The bartender poured the shots, which Lily downed immediately, shaking her head at the burn. Then, instead of pulling out some cash, she dropped her FBI badge on the counter. The bartender's eyes narrowed.

"Something we can help you with . . . agents?" The bartender was a dark-skinned man, his eyes studying them. It was clear that he wasn't exactly thrilled that a couple of people were snooping around in his bar.

"We're trying to find a man named Jose Alvarez," Lily said. "Have you ever heard of him?"

The bartender leaned back, crossing his arms over his broad chest. He glared at them for a moment too long before he said, "I can't help you. I'm sorry." He had a Barbados accent, Lily noted, and he was a handsome man. Just her type. Which made Lily almost feel bad for going bulldog on him.

"If you know where Mr. Alvarez is," Lily said, "we need you to tell us. Now. I would hate to get additional law enforcement here."

The bartender only looked irritated. "If that is what you want, fine. But I am not going to cooperate." He turned, fixing his bar with a more mechanical feel.

Xander's hand shot out and grabbed the bartender's shoulder. "Let's talk about this for a second, shall we?"

Lily felt herself tense up. He was too much of a loose cannon here. Maybe she just needed to go do the job alone, and then let him come back when the storm had passed. Maybe she should get him out of her hair—it seemed like a good idea. One look at Xander and she noticed something loosen in him too. Maybe he had the same thought.

"You think I'm going to help you ruin someone's life," the bartender spat, shrugging his arm away. "I don't think so, man."

"Why would you think we're going to do that?" Lily asked, although she had an idea. Law enforcement on the islands could be brutal. But they were with the FBI. They'd do it by the books. "Please," Lily added. "We just want to talk to him. It's important."

The bartender's brown eyes lingered on Lily's. She held eye contact firmly, empathetically, and hoped it'd get through to him.

Sometimes being all aggressive and haughty wasn't the way to get through to people. Sometimes, they just needed to be treated like people.

The bartender sighed, looking away. "What do you want to know about him?"

Lily allowed herself a quick half-smile, relieved. "Where can we find him?"

"If you wait a few hours, you should see him handing out fliers outside the club, spouting all his ideologies all over my customers."

Lily lifted an eyebrow. This wasn't what she was expecting. "I'm sorry—what do you mean?"

"I mean, the guy is a missionary of some kind," said the bartender.

Lily frowned. "A missionary? He's religious?"

"A missionary, I think. I don't know, I don't listen to him. He's always trying to convert someone."

Missionary . . .

That detail stuck out to Lily like a red alarm. Sophia Harris was from Utah. Her father was the governor there.

Utah happened to have an extremely large missionary population.

She shot Xander a look to see if he was thinking the same thing. He just nodded, and Lily hoped they were on the same page. She didn't know Xander well enough to predict his thought patterns yet; she didn't know how keen of a mind he had, but if he noticed that detail, too, it would go a long way in her building respect for him as an agent.

Until they could talk in private, she focused on the bartender. "When should he be here?"

"I told you, a few hours," he said. "After sunset."

Damn. They couldn't wait that long.

"Well, we ain't got all day," Xander said, echoing Lily's thoughts. "Any idea where this guy lives?"

"Of course not," the bartender shot back.

"I think you know more than you're telling," Xander said.

"You don't know that."

"Of course I do," Xander said. "Because by now you've made up your mind that you want to help us without getting your bar looked at a little more closely by local law enforcement."

"You are asking too much of me."

"And I am sorry for that," Lily cut in. "But we need to find Alvarez. Does he ever purchase anything here? Maybe you can give us his credit card number from your records."

The bartender's eyebrows pulled down, even as his mouth opened in surprise. "I'm sorry, I just don't think that is the right way to handle this."

"Then tell us where he lives," Xander cut in, his hands clenched into fists. "That's what you need to do."

"I told you, I don't know," the bartender said.

"Please," Lily said, looking up at him. She knew of the effect she could have on men sometimes, the look in her eyes that would normally get them to cave.

The bartender grunted in frustration. "If I help you, will you leave?"

"Hell yeah we will," Xander said.

Once more, the bartender's dark brown eyes warily eyed Lily. Then, with a sigh, he went to his till and opened a compartment that contained a printed record of sales.

Lily's heart picked up. He was helping. He was going to do it.

"He is the only one who pays for bottled water with a credit card." The bartender smoothed out a long receipt and scrolled down it. He stopped partway and showed it to Lily and Xander. Lily eagerly leaned forward.

There was a record for a bottle of water sale, and the credit card number was at the bottom.

Lily thought she could make out a name, but she couldn't quite read it.

"Do you have a pen?" she asked.

The bartender looked annoyed but went to the counter and grabbed one. He pushed it toward her, clearly not convinced they'd leave as they'd promised.

"Thanks." Lily grabbed the pen and immediately jotted down the credit card number on her notepad. Then, she tore off another piece of paper. She scribbled her number at the bottom, tearing it off before handing it to the bartender. "In case you change your mind about helping us. Please, call me."

Lily threw a fifty-dollar bill on the counter.

"For the tequila. And your time."

The bartender seemed reluctant to accept the money, but still took it and stuck it in a cash register.

"I'll be in touch," Lily said. She stood up, and so did Xander. They picked up their bags and headed toward the door.

"I don't think you'll hear from me," the bartender said.

Lily kept walking. That was fine—he'd given them what they needed.

Now, they could run his credit card through the system and track down where Alvarez was staying.

Hopefully, they'd have an address before this evening. That would allow them time to get surveillance on him, scope out the area, and feel out the exact best plan of action.

They'd do this all by the book.

If Alvarez was the killer, she and Xander would arrest the man and bring him in.

Nobody would have to die this time.

*

Moments later, Lily sat in the passenger seat of the rental car with the credit card number in front of her, phone pressed to her ear. Xander sat silently behind the wheel, but Lily sensed an antsy energy coming off him.

Finally, the local tech here on the island—Jennifer Gomez—answered, her voice coming through the phone, "What can I do for you, Agent Dawn?"

"I need you to run a credit card for me," Lily said.

"Sure, what's the number?"

Lily rattled off the number, then waited as Jennifer got to work. Lily glanced at Xander as she waited. He stared outside, into the parking lot of the club. Then, finally, Jennifer's voice came back. "Okay, I have a hit. A hotel in Freeport. The card was used there earlier today."

A hotel. That could be the answer.

Lily let out a sigh. "Great, thank you so much, Jennifer. One more thing—what name did he use?"

"Ah, that is where it gets trickier," Jennifer said. "It is not on the credit card statement. But he used Country Express. The CoEx system is different than the credit card system, and it will tell you the last name on the card. Normally."

Lily's heart started to race. "What does that mean?"

"There is no last name on the card. The only name attached to it is Jose. Obviously, from the store records, we know he is the one who bought it."

"Okay," Lily said, "Can you get the address?"

"Sure," she said, and a few moments later she was back, "I'm sending it to your phone."

"Perfect," Lily said. "Thanks, Jennifer."

"No problem, Agent Dawn. If you guys need anything else, let me know."

"I will," Lily said. "Thanks again."

"Anytime."

With that, Lily hung up and looked at Xander, who was staring at her, waiting. "You ready, Agent Jackson?"

CHAPTER NINE

Lily's fist pounded against the door of the hotel room Jose Alvarez was allegedly staying at. When they didn't instantly get an answer, Xander reached over Lily's head and banged even louder.

But an answer never came. No matter how hard they knocked, Jose Alvarez—if he was in there—was not coming to the door.

Then they heard movement on the other side. Something banging.

"He's in there," Lily muttered.

"Son of a bitch," Xander said, then banged again. "Jose Alvarez, this is the FBI! Open the damn door!" Xander reeled back and went to kick the door in, but it wouldn't budge. Lily stood back.

"We're gonna need to get the hotel staff to let us in."

"Good idea," Xander said. "But keep your gun ready. Just in case."

Lily nodded and jogged down the hallway to the hotel reception, which was also unmanned. She banged a fist against the desk, then cursed to herself when nobody came. But then, she saw an intercom machine sitting on the counter, and she pushed a button on it.

Ring. Ring.

The sound echoed down the quiet hallway, startling her. Lily hit it again and waited, but it seemed like they were on their own here. Until, finally, a voice came over the intercom.

"I thought you were on break?"

"This is the FBI," Lily cut in. "I need to get into Room 112, now."

There was a pause. "Just a second."

Within moments, a door opened down the hallway and a short, pudgy man came trudging toward them. "Hello!" He waved.

Lily held up her badge. "FBI. Room 112, now, please."

The man shrugged, a look of annoyance crossing his face. Then, he held up a key card. "You're welcome," he said, and he walked off without another word.

Lily and Xander exchanged a glance and nodded. They slipped along the wall to the door and tiptoed inside.

"Nothing here," Lily whispered.

The room was completely empty, though it showed signs of having been occupied: an unmade bed, a pair of shoes kicked haphazardly to the side, and a phone sitting on the bureau with a light blinking beside it as if a message had been left but not listened to.

"Shit," Xander said. "What the hell is in this room?"

Lily frowned. They had to be getting close. But maybe Jose was smart enough to cover his tracks.

She crept toward the bathroom, and that was when she felt it: a breeze.

Lily's pulse jumped. She ran into the bathroom and kicked in the door.

The window was wide open. Below it, a platform that could easily be jumped on.

And then, as she looked down, across the hotel yard, she saw him.

Jose Alvarez. And he clambered off the roof, landing on the lawn of the hotel.

"Come on!" Lily shouted back to Xander. Lily leapt out the window first, landing with a *thud* on the terrace below, and Xander landed right after her.

"Shit," Lily whispered. "He's getting away."

Xander grunted; he was already running after him, gun drawn. With a few quick steps, he joined Alvarez on the lawn and started to chase after him. "Stop!" he screamed. "Alvarez! You're under arrest."

Alvarez ran through the hotel grounds, dodging guests and going out the gates to the street beyond. Xander and Lily followed, running between the traffic of tourists and locals of the Bahamas that milled about. Alvarez took a sharp left turn around a corner and headed for a parking lot, weaving between cars and staying ahead of them.

"Someone stop him!" Lily shouted, her gun raised. But nobody on the busy street seemed willing to get mixed up in something like this. People gasped, looking around in confusion, but no one stopped Alvarez.

Alvarez kept running until he spotted a group of people on mopeds. Lily watched, grinding her teeth as Alvarez shoved an old woman off her moped and hopped on. With the advantage of a small vehicle, he drove off, ducking and weaving through pedestrians and traffic alike.

"Damn it!" Xander shouted.

Lily stormed up to the other people who were on mopeds. She felt bad about this, but she didn't have a choice.

"FBI—I'm sorry," she said, "but we're going to need to borrow these."

She and Xander hopped on the two mopeds. Within seconds, they were in pursuit of Alvarez.

As they pulled up behind Alvarez—jolting along through the crowded, but sunny streets—Lily felt her chest tighten. Alvarez was a block ahead of them, and he would get away if they didn't do something.

"You think you can catch him?" Lily hissed to Xander.

"Hold on," Xander said, and he gunned the moped forward, closing the space between them and Alvarez as quickly as possible. He hung back, though, just far enough that Alvarez wouldn't know he was there.

Alvarez reached the border of downtown Freeport, and then spilled out onto a highway, heavy with traffic. He was weaving through cars now, taking sharp turns at high speeds. Lily followed suit, but as they cut across lanes, they passed a cement truck and—before they could process what was happening—it sped into their path.

"Oh, god—Xander!"

They slammed on the brakes and swerved past, missing the cement truck by inches. It zoomed ahead of them and punched right through the storefront of a market. Products flew everywhere: cans of beans, bags of potatoes, boxes of cereal. Everything burst into pieces and rained down onto the highway.

Xander turned in behind a family's minivan, effectively hiding his moped from Alvarez's view. "Hold on."

Within seconds, Xander merged into traffic and built up speed. In front of them, Alvarez was still making a break for it, driving fast down the narrow street and weaving around cars at high speeds.

"Come on, come on," Xander muttered.

"What are you doing?" Lily wanted to ask if he was sure about this, but it was too late for questions.

Xander looked over at her and winked. Then, without any more hesitation, he kicked out and the moped leaped forward in a single burst of speed. Suddenly, his moped was flying onto the highway and heading toward Alvarez.

Lily wasn't about to fall behind. She pressed hard on the gas and made chase.

Xander swerved into traffic and cut off another moped; the riders cursed, flipping them off as he took over the lane. "Get out of here!" he screamed, but they ignored him completely and never even looked back as he weaved through the three cars, narrowly avoiding a minivan with a child inside.

Lily gaped at Xander in disbelief; she had no idea he was such a daredevil, but she wasn't going to let him get too far ahead. She was in this too—she had to catch Alvarez.

She stood on the gas and rocketed forward, swerving into traffic behind Xander.

They were getting closer to Alvarez; Lily could see him now, weaving forward through traffic. Her pulse raced. She had done her share of risky things in the FBI, but this was on a whole new level.

Xander was speeding toward Alvarez, and the gulf between them was closing quickly.

Alvarez was in Xander's blind spot now—he never saw him coming.

"Xander—" Lily said, an involuntary breath hitching in her throat. "Slow down."

"No time," Xander replied, his voice low and urgent beside her.

They narrowed the distance between them and Alvarez, whose head snapped up at the last second and saw them coming straight for him. He screamed in terror and veered sharply, trying to get out of the way of disaster—but it was too late. Xander's moped slammed into his hard and bounced off; Alvarez flew out of control, tumbling to the ground in a shower of heated sparks.

One heartbeat. Two heartbeats passed. Then: an explosion of excitement and adrenaline pulsed through Lily's veins as she watched Alvarez hit the pavement, hard, a hundred yards in front of her own moped. Xander's body ejected from his—but he landed on the grass with an expert roll. Lily skid to a halt up ahead as Alvarez now writhed in pain on the pavement. They were in a small shopping district, and people crowded around to see what was going on. Some went to help Alvarez, but Lily ran through the crowd with her badge up.

"FBI! Out of the way, please!"

On the grass nearby, Xander stood up and dusted himself off. Alvarez went to stand—to keep running—but his knee buckled, and he fell back down. He'd been injured in the crash.

Lily and Xander jogged toward him slowly. Alvarez was covered in scrapes from the fall, and his knee was badly twisted. He tried to push himself up, but he looked at Lily, who was walking directly toward him with an expression like she was going to skin him alive. Fear gripped his face, but he couldn't get up to run again—and Xander put a foot on his creaking knee, pinning him down.

"Jose Alvarez," Lily said coldly. "You have a lot of explaining to do."

He looked up at her, blood dripping from his scrapes. "I don't know what you're talking about. Why are you people chasing me?"

Lily walked over, standing above him with her handcuffs out. "I think the better question is, why were you running?"

Xander grabbed him and pulled him up, twisting him around. Jose barely resisted as Lily slapped the cuffs on him.

Now, all they needed was to get him to talk.

CHAPTER TEN

Lily was so accustomed to working in the United States that the architecture of the Freeport, Bahamas police station threw her off when she first saw it—with its all-white walls and blue awning, it had a different vibe altogether. The low, slanted building was mostly made of concrete, with long panes of glass and evenly spaced white pillars. The whole thing was covered in bright blue paint.

Looking into the interrogation room through the double-sided glass was all the same, though. Gray walls. No windows. A single table. On one side: two chairs. On the other: Jose Alvarez.

He'd been cagey since they brought him in. Now, Lily and Xander were doing their additional research before they continued with a full-blown interrogation.

Lily turned back to her laptop, which was sitting open on the table, showing everything the FBI had on Jose Alvarez. There wasn't much. He was a missionary born in Virginia who had been travelling with a missionary group to the Bahamas, and that was why he was here. He had no criminal record. But one thing Lily didn't get was—if he was travelling with the missionary group, why wasn't he with them now? He'd been here for a month, staying at that same hotel. It was a long, expensive, and lonely vacation, and Alvarez's credit card bill was raking up the cash.

"I think we should contact the head of this missionary group," Lily said to Xander. He was standing in front of the glass, watching and observing Jose. "We need to find out why he's not with them."

"I can call them, but I doubt they'll crack easily. They're probably very religious," he said, the irony in his tone not lost on Lily. They both knew what religious types were like when it came to protecting their own kind.

"It's fine," Lily said, taking out her phone. "I can call them."

In one smooth motion, Xander sat in front of her at the table. "I said I got it, Dawn."

Lily scowled. *What was his deal?* She thought they were past the whole "big man in charge" thing. "It's fine," Lily said, taking out her phone. "I've got this."

Xander narrowed his eyes at her, but she was already typing in the number. She made the call and waited. On the other end of the line, it rang and rang, until— "Hello?" It was a woman's voice.

"Hi, this is Agent Lily Dawn of the FBI calling about one of your missionaries. Are you Joan Tibbets?"

"How did you get this number?"

Lily paused, glancing at an annoyed-looking Xander. "Ma'am, I'm with the FBI. I need to talk to you about one of your members, Jose Alvarez."

"Oh, goodness. What has he done this time?"

Lily paused, taking that in. So, Jose had a reputation, even among the missionaries. "I'm calling to ask why he is not currently with your group."

"We couldn't have him any longer," she said. "He was making our female members uncomfortable."

Lily paused again. "Ma'am, what was he doing?"

"Well," she said magnanimously, "he was just always so attentive to women, you know? He'd get close to them and I know it's terrible, but we couldn't have it any longer. I mean, they even switched rooms because of him. And he had his own bank card! Just rubbing everyone the wrong way."

Xander raised an eyebrow at her, but Lily plowed forward. "I need you to answer a few questions if you could. Do you have any idea why he might have wanted to stay in Freeport?"

"No—I mean—maybe he likes coconut rum. Yes, that's it." She laughed condescendingly at her own joke.

"Was Jose ever violent toward the women?" Lily pressed. "What did he do exactly to make them uncomfortable? Was it sexual harassment?"

"He was always staring. Always trying to corner them. But we were able to talk him out of it—he finally respected that we were in charge, you know?"

Lily grimaced and nodded along as she waited for the missionary spokeswoman to take a breath. Xander had crossed his arms, and he cocked an eyebrow at her as she battled it through.

"Right," Lily said. "So, you've never had any problems with him before? He wasn't violent?"

"No. Just a pest, really."

Lily tried to wrap it up. "So, he was never violent with any of you?"

"No—we were able to get him to leave without any fuss at all. He was—if anything—insensitive. I mean, we all have our own god, but he acted like his was the only one worth knowing about."

Lily tried not to feel relieved about that—she was certainly relieved that Jose didn't hurt women—but she definitely did feel relief at that news.

"Thank you," Lily said, ready to hang up. "I really appreciate your help."

"No problem," she said, probably ready to put Jose out of her mind.

Jose Alvarez seemed like a womanizer, but he wasn't violent, and he wasn't here because he wanted to go on a religious pilgrimage. Whatever his motivations were, Lily didn't think religion had anything to do with it.

She turned back toward Xander, who was looking at Jose though the glass, a speculative look on his face.

"What are you thinking, Jackson?" Lily asked.

He looked back at her, his green eyes locking on hers. "Something's strange about all this. Why'd they even bring him on the trip if he made chicks uncomfortable? More importantly, why the hell would he stay here and blow all his cash on hotels, instead of just going back to the US?"

"Maybe so he could start a killing spree here in the Bahamas," Lily said, glancing at Jose. He was a tanned guy with a thin, black mustache, and he was only twenty-eight years old. "But what's more odd," Lily added on, "is that he was apparently handing out missionary fliers at the Rammer Jammer. Seems like an odd way to pick up women."

"Wonder if any of our victims ever crossed his path," Xander said.

Lily stood up, determined. "Only one way to find out. Let's get him to crack."

CHAPTER ELEVEN

Lily and Xander sat across from Jose in the interrogation room, but Jose wasn't budging. With his head hanging low, he kept quiet as they assaulted him with questions.

"Why did you stay in Freeport, Jose?" Lily asked.

No reply.

"Your whole team left without you," Xander added on. "Seems like you weren't too popular with the ladies."

That made Jose's nostrils flare. "What . . . what did they tell you?"

Finally, some words.

"We know all about you, Jose Alvarez," Lily said, leaning forward.

Jose's dark eyes darted between them as though he were trapped. Lily could practically see the gears in his head turning as he tried to figure out how they knew so much, what he could tell them, and if it was all worth it.

"What do you want?" he asked at last.

Lily looked at Xander, who nodded encouragingly at her. "Tell us everything from the beginning," she said neutrally.

"I was just on a Mission with church members is all. I never did anything wrong to those women—I just talked to them," Jose said. "They never liked me, ever since I got on the team. They wouldn't even give me a chance."

"Why not just go home instead of staying here in Freeport all by yourself?" Lily asked. "Surely it couldn't hurt to cut your losses and go back."

Jose shook his head, his hair bobbing through the air like a broken doll's. "No, no . . . I couldn't go back," he said quietly. "People would think I'm a coward. Like I just ran out on my father—like I was afraid of divinity."

Lily made her move then, dredging up what she knew they had on him already and tossing it out into the open between them like a poisoned dart.

"So, you moved here to target women outside of the US. To kill them. Didn't you, Jose?"

His brown eyes went wide. “Wait—what?”

Xander shot Lily a look. Maybe he hadn’t expected her to be so bold, but Lily wanted to gauge Jose’s reactions—see if she could spot guilt.

“I—I don’t know what you’re talking about,” Jose said. “Kill who? What do you want with me?”

Lily took out two photos from the file: one of Sophia Harris and another of Marie Levesque. She slapped them on the table and slid them toward Jose.

“You know these women, don’t you, Jose?”

“What? No!” He stared down at the photos, trembling.

Xander leaned forward, his jaw flexed. “Listen here, you dirty little son of a bitch. You come clean right now or I promise you, we will make sure you never step foot on US soil again. Is that what you want?”

Jose blinked rapidly at Xander like he was a giant bear. “I . . . I swear, I don’t know them!”

Lily and Xander exchanged a look of mutual disgust before Xander leaned back in his chair, trying to calm down. “Let’s walk through it together then,” Lily said, flipping a page in her notepad. “Tell me what you did this whole time you were in Freeport.”

Lily gazed evenly at him, her visage betraying nothing. She said nothing—she’d let Jose do the talking.

Lily watched Jose, whose hands were clenched in his lap as he tried to convince them of his innocence. She looked into his dark eyes and saw something there—something that confirmed what she already knew: he was not being honest with them.

Clearly the man had been living a lie all this time and now it was catching up to him. He was letting loose secrets that he’d kept bottled up inside him for years—secrets he thought could never come back to haunt him again. Lily and Xander had just cracked open a can of worms underwater, and Jose was going to have to talk, sooner rather than later. And it seemed like he’d figured that out because he finally started talking.

“I’ve been . . . I’ve been trying to build a new life here,” Jose finally stammered. “I wanted to start my own church.”

“That’s why you were handing out fliers,” Lily said. “Why the club?”

“I wanted to help the sinners!”

Xander let out a sarcastic laugh. "They're the sinners? Look at you, boy. Making ladies feel uncomfortable, and for what? Your own sick, sexual desires?" He slammed his hand on the table, making Jose jump. "Don't get off topic. Look at these two girls. You know them. Tell me about them."

"I don't know them!"

"Take a harder look, Jose." Lily inched the picture of Sophia closer to Jose. According to the hotel worker, Jose was seen harassing Sophia. He did know her. Lily just needed him to fess up. "You wanted this girl to join your church, didn't you, Jose?"

He looked closer.

"Think harder. You know her. She was at the beach, right?"

Jose's eyes throbbed with blood as he tried to recall his memory.

"I don't . . . I . . ."

"Thought you'd make her like you, huh?" Xander said.

Jose shook his head wildly, leaning back from the picture. "No, no . . . I . . ." He looked up at Xander and Lily, pleading with them.

"Just tell us what you did." Xander snapped. Jose jumped again, startled.

Lily gave him a new card to play: the victim. "She was on vacation alone," Lily said, her voice softening. "In fact, doing the same thing you were—trying to escape from all this." She gestured wildly, making her words mean nothing. "But now she's dead, Jose. Someone killed her."

She pulled out the photo of Marie Levesque, placing it neatly beside the other one on the table in front of Jose. His eyes went from one photo to another as he started to gasp for air.

Xander slammed his palm onto the table once again, making Jose jump so hard he knocked his chair back. "Don't play games with me, boy," Xander said, leaning over the table into Jose's face. "You chased them down until they died, didn't you?"

Jose shook his head—over-dramatized and completely unbelievable as though he had no idea what they were talking about. "I . . . I just wanted to talk to her about joining my new church," Jose said.

Xander rolled his eyes. "You're telling us you tried to convert some poor girl you met on the street when she turned you down? Couldn't have been pleasant for her. So, you killed them both because nobody liked you?"

Jose shook his head again, breathing deep and hard, trying to get his bearings back in his corner of this interrogation room. "It wasn't like that," he said at last. "It wasn't like that at all."

Lily leaned forward, planting her hands on the interrogation table between them. "So, what was it like then? Tell me Jose; give me the whole story."

He choked on his words for a long time before he fessed up.

"I . . . I wanted to save her," he said.

"Save who?" Lily asked. She couldn't believe this man; he was ready to confess but only with contradictions and half-truths. It was like she was sitting there with an amateur, and she was supposed to be the rookie.

"Her name was Sophia." Jose said, his voice harsh and hoarse. "She got on the bus when I . . . when I was riding through Freeport. And when she looked at me, those big brown eyes of hers were so sad . . ."

He fell into silence for a long time, wringing his hands together and staring down at the photo of Sophia Harris. Lily and Xander were silent, too, giving him time to collect his thoughts before he continued. But part of her felt that if she wasn't careful, Jose would clam up again.

"She got off here," he said finally. "And I talked to her." His eyes went out of focus as he looked over the desk, lost in a memory he could never take back. "She didn't seem so sad anymore."

Lily wondered if it was pity that prompted him to ask the girls to talk with him. Was it pity or maybe something darker? She wanted to hear Jose confess all of his crimes—every last one—but she knew it would take a bit more.

"I swear," he said, "I did not harm her! I may have become a little . . . obsessive when I was trying to convince her to join me, but I left her alone!"

"So, you didn't chase her down?" Lily said quietly, cocking an eyebrow. "You stayed away from her and never talked to her again?"

"And you didn't follow her to the hotel?" Xander asked.

His gaze went to the pictures on the table. "I don't know," he finally said. "I don't remember." His eyes lowered as if he regretted his weakness, but Lily knew that now was her chance to seal the deal.

"Listen, I'm rooting for you, Jose," Lily said, leaning closer, implying they were on the same side of the fence now. If she played this right, she just might get the confession out of him that Xander couldn't seem to get. "You admitted you've probably gone about this all wrong." She leaned forward until she got eye-to-eye with him and put a hand on his arm. "But somebody's dead because of whatever obsessions you had with these girls." Her voice became harsh once more, like she was scolding a child. "You have to tell us what happened."

He swallowed hard and nodded but slowed into another long silence as his eyes returned to Sophia's face.

She almost expected him to confess now. Play time was over.

But Jose said, "I am telling you, I did not hurt this girl. I followed her to the hotel, yes, but it was only to try to convince her to join and then she got scared of me."

Lily had enough of this. She pulled out the file and checked the details of Sophia's case. She was last seen alive at the hotel three days ago and was found dead the next morning, which meant Jose would need a rock-solid alibi if he were to be cleared.

"Where were you three nights ago, Jose?" Lily asked.

"I was, well, I was at the hotel."

"The hotel you can easily sneak out of," Lily said. She sighed, instead turning her focus to the more recent victim—Marie. The victim Jose seemed to not be reacting to. "Where were you last night and this morning then?" she asked. If he had an alibi for last night, then he might not be their guy.

"I . . . uh . . . I was . . ." he sputtered, broken words coming out of his mouth. "At my, well, I was trying to make some money, so I volunteered at a shelter in exchange for food. I slept there all night."

Xander gave a whimsical groan. "Locked doors, many witnesses?"

Jose shook his head rapidly. "Yes! Yes, exactly!" he said more confidently. "You can go talk to them if you'd like! It's where I always go when I'm stressed out."

"Well," Lily said, standing up and slowly stacking the pictures of Sophia and Marie behind her on her table, "We'll have to call them and figure that out."

*

"Well, that was a waste of my drinking time," Xander said as they stepped out into the hallway. He hooked his thumbs in his belt loops, looking pleased to be free of the interrogation room. He shrugged. "This guy's full of shit."

Lily's mouth hung open as she turned to Xander. "You're telling me you think he's our guy?" she said, nearly indignant. She had work on her mind when it came to this case. But asking the wrong questions and starting from the wrong angle could accidentally lead them miles away from catching their perp—no matter how stupid those questions might make her look to Xander and the department brass.

She pushed past him out into the hall like she had a place to be somewhere else—like she wasn't just trying not to punch Xander in the face right now. But she didn't have anywhere else to go, not until they had their killer behind bars.

"He's got no alibi for at least one of the deaths," Xander replied, taking off his hat and placing it on her head like a hat trick at the end of a magic show. "He's also painted himself a bit of a wuss with all that obsessing over these women." Xander glanced back at Jose's door as if remembering everything Jose had said.

"But if his alibi for Marie checks out, then it's probably not him," Lily reasoned. "Don't you think? Sophia and Marie were killed under the same MO—we're looking for one guy."

Xander shrugged, raising his hands up defenselessly. "If that's what you need to be sure, then we'll get an alibi for the last victim." Xander said. "But I wouldn't hold my breath. It's kind of sad that a guy like this waited this long to finally do something . . . only to be caught by a little girl like you."

Lily's blood burned. He really had a way of pissing her off. "Just focus on what you have to do," she replied, trying not to be provoked by his patronizing words.

"I meant it as in, he spent so much time harassing women, only to get taken down by one," Xander defended. "Not trying to bug you—this is just how I talk."

Lily turned away. "Whatever, Jackson. I'm gonna call in that alibi. You do . . . whatever it is you do."

With that, she took off. She needed a moment away from him to figure this thing out.

CHAPTER TWELVE

His boat moved slowly along the coastline, and he peered out at sea with a pair of binoculars pressed to his eyes. Through the lenses, he made out her form; a pretty girl, lounging on her yacht, all alone.

Where are your friends, little girl?

He couldn't help but smile. This girl was so young, certain of herself, even in her own isolation. But where were her friends? Where was her family? It didn't matter; he wasn't looking for them.

Putting down the binoculars, he went back to handle his boat. The sea was so azure around him as the sun set, and the trees of the Bahamas fanned over the sand on the beach ahead. The tall, skinny pines were like the spokes of a giant umbrella. They were like green suns reflecting light, and the day's work was done. The people of the island country came down to the beach below their homes and their hotels to swim and picnic, to play in the surf and sand, to dance and laugh in the long shadows. Their cabanas were built of wood and painted bright colors: blue, red, and yellow. And they walked barefoot down wooden planks over soft sand. Such a beautiful place, this was. Janie had loved it here.

Such perfect peace.

The sky was getting dark, but the boat moved slow. Soon, the girl would realize it was getting late and get up to steer her boat back to shore.

That was when he'd strike.

Far across the water, up in empty space, he felt the briefest of sensations. A scan passed over his universe, like a descending mile-long fingernail tickling the cosmic tapestry above. Nothing to see here: just a sliver of broken space, a single anomaly. Unimportant, even. It would be striking more soon, though; it would be striking all over the planet.

It happened all the time.

He'd thrust towards her in the dark of night, silent as a shark.

There was still plenty of time. This would make his third kill. His third star. She was a perfect addition to the map he was creating.

For a moment, he paused and lowered his binoculars. He let out a sigh, and then his eyes began scanning the panorama before him. The islanders close by were lit like fireflies, but the larger crowds from the nearby hotels were visible farther away, blotches of orange and red in the radiating streetlamps. Yes. Tonight was perfect for a hunt.

Staring out across these throngs, a smile widened on his face.

They look down and are jealous of my power when they see my stars, he thought. *And yet they do not understand it; they do not know who I am . . . And that will be their downfall.*

Slowly, he leaned back into his captain's chair and picked his binoculars back up.

Staring out towards the misty horizon, he began to plot his next move.

The wind was on his back. The sky was on his hand. He was a part of nature, not a part of man.

Or so he told himself, anyway.

The breeze kicked up, and waves flowed under the wind's pressure. And he knew it was because of him—as if he were breathing and living through this world instead of just existing in it.

This was no gift from God, not in any conventional way. It was not a blessing or some arbitrary talent like laughter. It was all him, it always had been. And best of all, it didn't feel like "him." He remembered what it had felt like to be a boy in silent awe, experiencing life firsthand and taking everything in. He'd been like this again for so long. Perhaps that was why this place still held some sort of fascination for him, even though he could no longer remember who he'd been or why it had happened. All he knew was this new path, this new journey to connect star and sea.

He watched the girl, knowing that she would be his salvation, and he would be hers.

He would make her a star. Something permanent. Something no one would ever forget.

CHAPTER THIRTEEN

Lily pushed open the door to their rental house. She had been dreading the moment she'd have to come back to this shared house with Xander and deal with his attitude in a more closed setting. But it was late now, the sun was setting through the curtains, and they'd run out of leads.

Jose Alvarez was a dead end.

His alibi had checked out.

While he couldn't necessarily be placed for the night Sophia died, he did have a rock-solid alibi for when Marie did.

He wasn't their guy.

And that frustrated Lily more than anything. They'd wasted so much time on him. It pissed her off.

She threw her purse on the console table and brought her laptop into the open concept living room. The walls were more window than wall, and beyond the glass, Lily couldn't help but appreciate the beauty of the emerging stars.

"Sheesh, darling," Xander began, stretching his limbs as he sauntered toward the kitchen, which was also open concept and had marble countertops. "I'm starved. You ever eat?"

She shot him a glare as she sat down on the white couch. "Of course I do. I'm starving too."

He opened the fridge. "Any weirdo dietary restrictions?"

Lily lifted an eyebrow. "What, you're going to cook?"

He shot her a grin over his shoulder. "Do I look like I can't cook?"

She rolled her eyes. He truly was irritating. Lily opened her laptop, unbothered. "I'm pescatarian," she said. "Fish only. No meat."

Xander chuckled. "I knew you were that type of chick."

Lily had no time for this. Why did he always have to go there? Was it really that much of a joke to him? Her lips twitched. "Know a lot about me, don't we?"

"I'm an observant guy," he said, grabbing some ingredients. She shot him another glare. The man was insufferable . . .

But he was making her dinner too. Chef Xander was actually cooking for her? She just had to hope he didn't poison her food. Either way, it was nice to know she could focus on the case.

She needed to know more about Marie Levesque. She was more than just the heiress of a huge company in France, she had a life. She had a life in America.

Lily checked Marie's social media accounts to get a better sense of who she was in her life.

Some of her posts were in French, but Lily could gather that Marie was popular in France for being rich. She also liked sports. And she ran an after-school program called "All We Need To Be Heroes."

That was interesting.

"So, what have you learned about our victim?" Xander asked. The aroma of garlic and cooking fish filled the house. Lily had to admit, it made her mouth water.

"I'm just looking through her social media," Lily said, scrolling. "She had a lot of friends and pretty photos. She wasn't an influencer like Sophia, though. I wonder why she was travelling alone."

"Who knows," Xander said. He opened the windows in the house. The air was hot and breezy as it swept through the house. She liked this part of the island country, there was a sense of peace out here in the middle of the gulf. And there was something about the ocean at night as if it held secrets. She couldn't help but feel that waves could split open at any moment and reveal some dark mystery. A mystery she hoped wouldn't be trapped in those deep blue waters forever.

But they needed answers now. And surely, there was someone out there who could answer their questions about Marie better than anyone.

Xander's voice cut Lily off. "Order up," he said. Xander plated some food and came over to Lily with two heaping bowls of seafood pasta. He set them down on the coffee table, then sat on the loveseat. Lily had to admit—the food looked great. Colorful and red.

Lily wasn't about to argue.

She began to eat, her stomach grumbling. She hadn't eaten since earlier in the day. There had been no time, with them running all over town chasing leads. They were so close to closure. So close to justice.

But they had to eat first. They needed their strength. As she was working on the fish, she leaned over her laptop, which she had propped on the coffee table, and continued looking.

Lily stopped on a photo of Marie with her arms around her father, smiling brightly.

"We need to talk to her family," Lily said, thinking out loud. "Namely, her father. They seemed close."

"Think we can get him on the line?" Xander asked. "He's some French billionaire, right?"

"Yeah, but he lives in the US. He could be on his way here, for all we know." Lily set her food aside as she found Lyam Levesque's number in the system. Xander finished his bowl and tossed it on the coffee table.

"You're on cleaning duty, though," he said to her.

Lily ignored him and dialed in the number. She placed her phone face-up on the table and put it on speaker, letting it ring and ring.

The first time, there was no answer.

She decided to try again. After all, this was a matter of time. They couldn't let the trail go cold. The best window for talking to him would be the present.

"Hello?" an older, gruff voice laced with a French accent finally answered.

Lily started as she sat up on her elbows, unable to hold her pose anymore. "Mr. Lyam Levesque," she said, her tone sharpened. "This is Agent Lily Dawn of the FBI, here with my partner, Agent Xander Jackson. We're looking into your daughter's case."

"I assume you have some news on that matter . . ." Lyam trailed off.

She stole a look to Xander, who looked back evenly with curiosity in his eyes.

"Not yet, sir," Lily said. "We were hoping to learn more about your daughter from you. Are you on your way to the Bahamas?"

"I can't just hop on a flight and—" He took a deep breath. Xander and Lily exchanged a look. His daughter was dead, and he couldn't hop on a flight? Then Lyam said, "My daughter needs to be returned home. We will bury her here, in America. She loved it here."

"Right, well . . ." Lily paused. "Unfortunately, Marie's body is still needed here for forensic analysis. We are trying to find out what happened to her. We do suspect homicide."

There was a brief pause at the other end of the phone.

"Homicide? You think someone killed my daughter?" he asked, in a small voice. "That doesn't make sense."

Xander shifted next to her. "Mr. Levesque, why'd your daughter go to the Bahamas?"

There was another pause. "She wanted to be independent. It was her idea to go stay at the hotel alone. She thought she would be going on some big adventure."

Lily frowned, and then reflected this to Xander with a shrug of her shoulders.

Xander stepped up, his voice softer now. Obviously, that made a difference in getting answers from this man. "And she had no plans to meet anyone here?"

"No. She wanted to go alone."

Lily and Xander exchanged another glance. "Can you tell us more about Marie?" Lily asked, straightening up a little bit. She did not want to think her question sounded like his daughter was just a case, but it was hard not to feel that way, sometimes.

Lyam said, "Marie was a sweet girl . . . strong headed but also compassionate. She was my princess." His voice cracked with emotion.

"You were close," Lily realized, looking to Xander as well.

"Anyone else in particular that she was close to?" Xander asked.

"Well, yes." It sounded like Lyam swallowed the word. "There was someone . . . Marie had a friend here. His name is Patrick Vance. He was more like a boyfriend, really, although they didn't label it."

Lily paused as she took note of that name on her electronic tablet, which sometimes served as her notebook. Patrick was nowhere near the Bahamas when Marie died, but Lily made a note to see if the boyfriend had any useful information about Marie. She always felt it best to know victims inside and out, as much as it sometimes hurt to learn all the intimate details of the people that she couldn't save.

"There's another thing," Lyam said, and Lily shot Xander a look. "My daughter loved sailing. It's part of why she was planning to go to the Bahamas."

"Sailing? Was she a sailor?"

"She loved boats. For her birthday, I bought her a yacht, thinking it would be fun for her to have one of her very own when she turned twenty-one. We just celebrated it a few weeks ago, and I gave her the present early even though her birthday is next month. She got it delivered to Freeport so she could use it there." His voice trailed off. He must also be aware that his daughter would never see that age now.

Lily took a deep breath and steered the conversation back on track. "Did Marie have any plans to sail here?"

"Most likely, but I'm not sure," Lyam said. "It's what makes the whole thing even more impossible for me to believe."

Xander took over again, saying, "Is there any way your daughter could've changed her plans between you last seeing her and when she arrived at the hotel? Any way she could've made plans with someone else?"

Lyam answered even before Lily had fully finished translating this question for him into French. "I don't know," he said with finality, his voice slightly shaky. "I wasn't privy to every detail in her life."

Lily sighed. It seemed like there wasn't much else Lyam could do for them now.

"Thank you, sir," Lily said. "We'll be in touch."

"Please find out who did this to her."

With that, the call ended. Lily and Xander sat on the couch in silence for a moment, unsure what to say. Lily felt for Lyam, losing his daughter must not have been easy. She thought of her own father, how devastated he'd been when Kara went missing and more recently, when she was declared legally dead, despite a body not being found.

It had been a nightmare.

Through the windows, it was completely dark now. At that moment, tiredness hit Lily's body. She looked at the mess Xander had made in the kitchen and sighed. She had to clean it up, then she had to sleep in this place for the first time.

Lily looked at the laptop screen, still with a picture of Marie Levesque open on it. Her heart pulled.

What happened to you?

"Let's hit the hay and start fresh in the morning," Xander said, standing. "I'm thinking that thing about Marie sailing could be something."

Lily was thinking the same thing. As much as Xander irked her, his instincts seemed spot on so far.

Accepting that there was nothing else they could do tonight, Lily got up. Tomorrow, they wouldn't waste any more time.

Tomorrow, they would find answers.

CHAPTER FOURTEEN

Lily settled into her bed on the upper level of the rental home. It felt more like a loft, which, in a way, reminded her of the bedroom she had growing up in Aruba. The blankets were white and fresh, and the mattress was surprisingly comfortable.

Still. Alone in the dark, with the moonlight seeping through the curtains, she found herself feeling extremely alone.

Xander was downstairs sleeping, but that didn't comfort her at all. Lily was a long way from trusting him.

For the first time in a long time, Eduardo slipped back into her mind. She didn't regret leaving him. Sometimes it did get lonely, though. Lily's only family were her parents who, obviously, did not speak to her. And Kara was gone. As much as Lily didn't want to accept that fact, it was true.

She turned over and faced the window, looking out at the moon over the sea. At least it was beautiful here.

Lily shut her eyes, allowing herself to drift away. She listened to the waves lap against the shore. This was the closest she'd been to home in years. As grim as this case was, Lily couldn't help but feel like fate had brought her back to the Caribbean.

Something shifted in her room. Lily's eyes popped open. She'd thought she'd heard something.

Creak.

Movement.

Lily's heart sped up.

She'd locked the door. Xander had a key, but he was downstairs.

Lily checked under her pillow. Her gun was there, and she gripped it tightly in her hand. She inhaled and got ready to spring up and make the shot if necessary—but then her hand yanked back, finding that the intruder was already in the room with her.

Her body froze, heart pumping even faster. She saw a shadow lurking against the wall, muddied and unclear in the darkness. Lily held her breath until she heard ragged breathing near her face and felt gusts of air cooling against her skin. Her eyes widened as the shadow moved closer.

Someone was in here.

Her eyes caught movement again. A shadow, sliding across the room, just below the window beside her bed.

Lily's breathing became shallow as she watched the shadow stop at the foot of her bed. Someone was in the bedroom with her. There was no reason for it, too, as far as she knew. Lily hated being this afraid, but then again, it wasn't every day that someone entered your room without permission.

Creak.

Movement again. Lily kept watching. The shadow stopped right next to the bottom of the bed. It didn't move any further. It just sat there, not more than two feet away from her own body.

"Xander?" Lily whispered, barely audible in her shaky voice. "Is that you?"

There was no response at first and then . . .

"Lily . . ."

Kara's voice.

Terror squeezed at Lily's heart. "Kara . . . no . . . you're gone."

It was a dream. It had to be. But Lily couldn't wake up. She'd heard her sister's voice.

Without warning, the shadow on the floor shifted, sliding upwards and across the floor until it was directly behind Lily's head. Without thinking, Lily twisted her body around and quickly looked behind her, but it was gone. Nothing was there except the darkness.

The bedsheets beneath her had slowly become damp. A film of sweat covered Lily's skin. She panted, trying to catch her breath in this short moment of wakefulness before . . .

It couldn't be her imagination. It was too real.

"You're not here . . ." Lily said, not even sure who she was trying to convince. It felt as though the wind had been blocked from her lungs as she lay frozen, staring as the shadow under the bed moved slightly.

"I am here."

That was Kara's voice, but it couldn't be real. Kara was gone. This was how Lily had wanted it, wasn't it?

"No," Lily whispered. "You're not here."

The silence dragged on. Seconds passed endlessly.

"I am here," Kara whispered finally, her breath suddenly hot against Lily's ear. "I am real, Lily. You left me behind."

"No!" Lily screamed in the dark, fighting an invisible force demanding she speak to it. "This can't be happening! You're gone!"

"Lily!" The voice grew stronger now, pushing against her will. "I'm back!"

"No!" she pushed out as loud as she could, against the ghostly hands pulling down hers. "This isn't real! Kara is dead!"

But there was no arguing with a dream, especially when it involved one of the unconscious with such intensity and raw emotion like this one. The shadowy hands pressed Lily's gun down toward her thighs and toward her waist band. She pushed them away, and the gun flew across the room.

Lily couldn't see her, but she felt the shadow. It was Kara. Somehow, in her dream state, she knew.

Lily awoke with a start when she heard a bang. Drenched in sweat, she looked around the empty room. Through the window, the sun was starting to rise.

There was no more shadow.

Lily's heart pounded. What the hell did she just experience? It had felt so real, so—

The banging continued. And that was when she realized that someone was knocking on her door.

"Dawn, you awake in there?" Xander called.

Lily took a few deep breaths. Why the hell was he knocking on her door so early?

"Coming," Lily croaked. She climbed out of her bed and straightened her clothes, trying not to show how rattled she had become by that dream.

It was just a dream. Kara wasn't—couldn't be there. She pulled it open and Xander peered in.

"You're not gonna like this," he said, leaning against the doorframe. Lily's heart dropped.

"What the hell do you mean?"

Xander let out a sigh. "They've found another body."

CHAPTER FIFTEEN

The speedboat cut through the water, and cool air hit Lily's face as the rising sun turned the sky blue. The coast guard had been waiting at the shore to pick up Lily and Xander as soon as they were ready—and now here they were, soaring across the ocean, toward where the next body was found.

Lily felt like the world had toppled on her head. This guy—this killer—he was accelerating. And he was doing it fast. She thought she'd have more time to track him down.

Now, another young girl was dead.

Lily didn't know who she was yet. The sound of the speedboat's engine was loud, and Lily, along with Xander and the two coast guard officers, were quiet. Lily turned to see Xander leaning against the boat with his aviators reflecting the morning light. Then, she turned back to the sea in front of her, a bad feeling churning deep in her gut.

This wasn't going to be pretty.

The last two girls were found off the coast in Freeport, but this one was a little farther out, beyond the city border, but still out in the water.

"Another girl," Officer Chandler said, as though reading her mind. The officer was cautious, and he kept watching her. "Looks the same as the last two."

Lily's eyes swept over the water. They would reach the site any minute now. She swallowed. "I need to see it for myself," Lily said finally. It felt like her voice was made of dust.

It took a few moments before they reached their destination, or at least what Lily assumed to be their destination: a boat, floating aimlessly in the water, surrounded by two other coast guard boats and an additional civilian boat. The two coast guard officers exchanged a glance as they slowed down, engine blazing as they neared.

"The witness found the boat floating at sea," Officer Chandler told Lily as he steered the speedboat toward the area. "Well . . . you'll get the rest of the story soon."

Lily didn't like the sound of that.

The speedboat drifted near another boat, and a big coast guard officer jumped onto the deck of the other boat to secure the boat to the other one. He pulled them close enough until Officer Chandler was able to jump out and pull the boat alongside them. Standing on deck, Lily started to feel uneasy. Xander appeared beside her. She could see a shaking, distraught-looking man talking to two other coast guard officers, and there were some Freeport police officers as well, all standing on the boat.

A sick feeling settled in the pit of Lily's stomach as she stepped off the speedboat onto the other boat.

"Where is she?" she asked, her voice gravity-less.

The man pointed. "There."

He looked just about ready to topple over. His eyes were bloodshot, and his face was drained of color. She thought he'd be too distraught to say anything at all, but he replied in a trembled voice, "Right there . . . on the floor."

He motioned toward the back of the boat. The two coast guard officers pulled up their skiff and tied it off to one side. Lily's stomach lurched when she saw it—a blue tarp flat on the floor at the back edge of the boat, and a young girl lay on top of it. Pale-skinned. Dark-haired. Soaking wet.

"Jesus," Xander said.

Lily bit the inside of her cheek, bracing herself to uncover the girl's face and look into her eyes. It was hard—God, was it hard—when she looked down at her face.

She couldn't be more than twenty years old.

"Goddammit," Lily murmured under her breath as she put a hand on top of the victim's head, brushing away some wet hair from her forehead and revealing her eyes, pale brown and glazed over like a doll's.

Lily knelt closer. There were slight ligature marks on her neck.

"She was found floating out beside her boat." Lily turned to see a coast guard officer—a tall, hulking, tanned man with tribal tattoos, clearly a Bahamas native. "But we cut her free."

"Cut her free?" Lily asked.

The officer stepped up and sighed, hands on his hips as he looked down. "It's real grim. That over there is her boat." He pointed to the pearl-white speed boat that was anchored off to the side. "It seems like she was rammed into. Our witness over there found the boat floating around, then he saw the body and called us."

"So, she's not supposed to be here," Lily murmured, glancing back at the victim. "She was taken out of her boat and dumped, then you brought her here."

The coast guard officer sighed. "I'm afraid so. We couldn't just leave the body in the water." He nodded toward the offender who had been in the boat. "That guy over there? His name is Patrick Stevens, nicknamed Spider—no idea why he's called that. He found her floating nearby and reported it to the police, then joined forces with them. Left his boat here too."

Lily pulled herself up from her scouring of the victim—she did that as a way to give herself a moment to start processing everything so she could focus on the matter at hand. The perpetrator was escalating.

"What do we know about the victim?" Lily asked, although she could already guess—a young woman, travelling to the Bahamas alone. This killer had a type.

"Uhh . . . we don't have much, just a name." The officer looked nervous. "Her ID was in her purse. She's Megan Frost—a UK resident. I've sent a message to the Freeport Police," the coast guard officer said. "They'll have all the details on her once one of their officers gives me a call back."

In the meantime, Lily would assume she was a traveler just like the other two girls. That is, before she was taken from her boat and murdered.

Lily looked back down at the victim. The girl didn't look familiar.

She felt a flash of anger rush through her heart. This was like looking into their eyes while they were alive, alive and just starting their lives . . . like Kara . . . and then gauging them over and watching them die because of some sick bastard.

"Damn," Xander said quietly beside Lily. He knew it too.

Lily gripped the metal bar on the side of the boat, shaking off waves of frustration. She had to focus. She couldn't dwell on that now. If they let themselves get lost in anger now, they'd lose track of their duties. Nothing mattered more than finding out who was doing this.

Lily turned back to the witness, who was still being questioned by the other two officers. Lily and Xander went up to him.

"You're Patrick Stevens?" Lily asked.

"Y . . . yeah," he said. "You can just call me Spider."

"We'll pass on that one," Xander said. "Mr. Stevens, why don't you tell us what you saw?"

"I d . . . don't know," he stammered. "I w . . . was just going to work—I sail on the weekend. I was heading back for today and when I saw her boat, floating out there on the water . . ." He turned to look at it—the speed boat glistened in the sunlight. "I had to check it out, right? So, I stopped my boat and went out of the side, but . . . she was floating there. I didn't realize that until I got over there." He shook his head. "She was dead—there was nothing I could do but call the police."

"Did you notice anything else—anyone else in the area?" Lily asked him.

"No . . . uh . . . no I don't think so," he stammered.

He seemed legitimately scared, horrified even.

"You don't think so?" Xander asked.

Spider shook his head. "I d . . . don't know. I was just trying to help her."

"Okay," Lily said. "That's fine. Agent Jackson and I are going to take a look around the victim's boat just to be sure. We'll be right back after that."

Lily followed Xander. They hopped off the current coast guard boat and onto the victim's boat, which the coast guard had moored to them. They looked around the small boat, going along the edge where they both stood on the side of the boat and leaned over, peering at it. She looked at the hull of the boat—there was no sign of damage from being rammed into, no visible damage from being attacked anyway.

"Looks fine to me," she called out to Xander as he poked around with a pole.

"Same," he called back after a moment—he had been grunting, poking around at the bottom of the boat for any kind of evidence. Lily reached over her shoulder for her badge, looping her thumb through the chain that would weight it down in her back pocket and pulling the chain tight so it wouldn't flop around when she walked.

"Well, I guess maybe she didn't notice anything either," Xander said when they were done, scratching his chin and sighing as they stood up, trudging away from the edge and looking over at Spider and Officer Chandler, who was still asking the man questions, on the other boat.

It seemed that he wasn't lying, but there was something off about all of this.

Mr. Levesque had said that Marie was into sailing. Now, here they were, on the boat of another girl—another victim—who obviously enjoyed it too.

This definitely felt relevant. But Lily needed to know more.

She kept scouring the boat for anything. It was a small yacht, and inside the cabin, there was nothing but a bottle of water and a towel. It seemed that Megan didn't pack heavy.

Lily went over to the hatch at the front of the boat, and that was when she realized that it was slightly open. Frowning, she knelt down and slowly lifted it up. Nothing seemed to be wrong until she looked at the hatch itself.

One side had a plastic piece to hold it in place, but the other did not. There were screw holes left behind. It looked like something was missing—one of the parts of the hatch.

"Hey," she said, looking up at Xander. "Come here."

Xander came over while Lily continued to feel around inside the hole. This was more than just broken pieces –someone had really tampered with this. The whole thing seemed jiggly, loose even, like the rest of the boat didn't match up with it.

"Weird," Xander said. "Could've been like this before—we can't rule that out."

"I know," Lily said, "but it seems odd. The rest of the boat is in perfect condition."

"So maybe the killer took a souvenir?" Xander asked.

Lily stood up and dusted herself off. "We need to find out where that part went."

*

Lily stepped off the boat, back onto the dock on the bay at Freeport, with Xander at her side. Megan's body was being taken to the coroner's, and hopefully, soon they would have a cause of death. Although with all the girls, it seemed to be drowning. The only thing that stood out to Lily were the ligature marks—however, they were too faint to suggest the girls had been strangled. Still, it raised a question: why were they even there? She hoped the coroner would get some answers.

For now, she wanted to track down that missing boat part. They made their way toward their rental house and went in through the sliding back door.

"Where should we go?" Xander asked. Lily had gone over to her desk, where her computer sat with the computer case open underneath it. She quickly fired up her computer, and after some time, went to Google and searched it, searching for any sites that sold boat parts and updates on the Freeport yacht club. Xander stood next to her and looked down at the screen while she searched.

Megan's yacht was US made. In her research, Lily discovered that there were parts on the boat that weren't manufactured—or even included—on boats that came from the Bahamas. So, if the piece was missing, why take it?

She heard Xander sigh and looked over to see that he had leaned back against the wall and had closed his eyes, breathing in deeply through his nose and letting it out slowly. She turned her attention back to her computer, scrolling down until she found a number for the Freeport yacht club.

"Let's call," she said, clicking on the number. The phone rang three times before it was picked up.

"Freeport yacht club."

"Hi, my name is Agent Lily Dawn of the FBI," she said, " We're trying to track down information on a piece that may have been stolen from a local yacht."

The man on the other end sighed. "Have you notified the police?" He asked.

"Yes," Lily said. "They're investigating it alongside us."

"Well, tell me about the part," said the man.

"It came from the underside of a hatch door. There were meant to be two of them, but one was missing."

"Ah, yeah, it sounds like that would help keep the door shut. A rare piece over here. It could be worth something to the right bidder, although without its twin, I doubt it's worth much."

Even odder that it would be missing, Lily thought. *Maybe whoever took it wanted to sell it anyway.*

"Thank you. Has anyone come in with a part such as this?"

"Not at all, ma'am, and we don't sell used parts here."

"Do you know where we might find someone who does?"

"Well . . ." The man cleared his throat, suddenly sounding uneasy. "I will say, there's a little island just off the coast—it's called Eagle Eye."

Eagle Eye. Lily had never heard of it.

"There are some guys there who work on boats, and it's sort of an under the table thing," said the man. "They are a bit of a seedy bunch, so I would be careful going in there."

Lily paused, her heart picking up. "Are they criminals?"

"Not that I know of," the man said. "Just a bunch of rough and tumble guys who enjoy the sea. But they don't like any kind of government intrusion."

"Our investigation is completely confidential," said Lily. "We're not here to judge."

"I'll let you try it, but I hope you know what you're getting into." The man sighed. "Anything else I can help you with?"

"No," Lily said, "but thank you for your help." She hung up the phone and took a moment to breathe.

"What is it?" Xander asked.

"There's an island not far from here, close to Freeport," Lily said, "where there are some guys who are known for . . . helping out with things. Or at least, fixing things that cannot be fixed."

Xander frowned. "Well . . ." He paused. "Let's get going."

Lily nodded. It wasn't much of a lead, but it was the best they had.

CHAPTER SIXTEEN

His head was spinning. This was too much for him—he needed too many girls if he was going to finish this celestial task, and he was running out of options. As he sat on his boat underneath the warm morning sun, he took out his phone and looked at the itinerary of the cruise ship.

It was a bigger vessel than he'd dealt with before. The more bystanders there were, the more dangerous his plan would become. He had to be careful. He had to play it safe.

But this was his best option. He needed more girls, and a cruise ship from America was perfect. It was full of college-aged beauties coming to party in the Bahamas.

It had to be full of easy targets. It would be too risky for him to hit a hotel or a resort—he'd just get caught. No, the mainland is too confined; the college girls would be staying at a bunch of different hotels. They'd be spread out and harder to keep track of. But on a cruise ship? They'd all shipped out together. One big target, one big cluster of young college students.

This would be his ticket. His way to complete the pattern. Four more would do, but he had to work one step at a time—he could not get caught. He could not let anything get in the way of his cosmic fate, his destiny.

He would complete the constellation.

He had only hours before the ship's arrival. But this time, he would think things through carefully. This time, he would not lose his cool and make mistakes. This pattern was taking shape in his mind more clearly now, tapping into the subconscious drive that had made him who he was. He was finally beginning to understand what was happening to him.

He was going to bring his daughter, Janie, home. This was how.

She'd been lost at sea, but he knew she was still out there. At night, she would be trying to navigate the stars like he'd taught her to. She was so smart. She didn't need a phone like the other girls her age. She had listened to his teachings when he took her sailing and showed her the way of the sky.

However, she needed him there to guide her right. Away from the grip of the Other, in order to come home.

The Other would not let go that easily. It had taken their mother away first to become a star in its own celestial pattern. The Other was holding Janie captive in another constellation, teaching her evil things and making her serve him. He had to set her free; he had to save her.

He'd been trying to reach her for so long. He'd been trying to save her ever since she slipped through his arms and disappeared into the sea. His sweet girl, gone from this world at just sixteen years old. He couldn't lose her again—he couldn't. He needed to bring her home.

He had to find the rest of the girls who would help him guide her home. He didn't know why he felt responsible for them, but he did. Somehow, he knew that these young beauties would ultimately be able to bring his daughter home.

And it was up to him—the Oceanic Guardian—to do what must be done to assist them in their journey, their quest to find their way back home.

The Universe had brought him here and now, given him a chance to get his daughter back. It was his first real task as the all-powerful visionary. He would only later learn how much of an impact he'd had.

This time, he would not repeat his mistakes. This time, he would get it right.

But for now, he could bide his time. Take it slow.

He shut off his phone and leaned back on his boat. Then, he picked up his rope and began practicing his knots.

He would need to be ready, after all.

CHAPTER SEVENTEEN

The sound of the water slapped against the edge of the dock as Lily approached. It had been a couple of years since she'd last driven her own boat, and she had missed the feeling of water below her as she soared forward. This was the Freeport Police's boat, and it was docked near the end. She stroked her hand along its hull and shivered when the smooth wood passed over splinters and old paint chips. It reminded her of her father.

This wasn't the time for a trip down memory lane, though. They needed to get to Eagle Eye and find out what was going on there. If the killer was there.

"All right, Dawn, strap in," Xander said, hopping into the boat and getting behind the wheel.

Lily stood there on the dock for a moment, dumbfounded. "Jackson, you're out of your mind if you think I'm letting you drive. I'm from the islands. I know how to drive a boat."

"Oh, yeah?" Xander said, amused. "I ride jet skis through electrical storms. This is child's play."

"Are you done?" Lily snapped.

They were still having problems communicating in each other's presence. Lily was trying to stay professional—to remember she was an FBI agent, and that he was her equal—but Xander Jackson really did have a way of getting under her skin.

She sighed when he put his hands behind his neck, leisurely, clearly enjoying pissing her off.

"Can I please just drive the boat?" Lily asked

Xander stood up and chuckled. "That's all you had to say, Captain."

Lily resisted rolling her eyes as she hopped on board. "Thanks," she muttered as he moved out of the way, letting her take the wheel.

Xander sat down beside her and smirked. "I hope you don't crash it—you could owe me big time if that happens," he said.

Lily tried to maintain her composure. "Just shut up and get ready."

He sat down next to her, and she caught the lingering smell of his cologne. Without thinking, she stole a glance at his profile. An intrusive thought hit her; he wasn't a bad-looking guy, as annoying as he was.

"What?" he asked.

Lily shook her head. "Nothing." With a single turn of the key, the motor roared to life and the boat began making its way towards Eagle Eye Island. Glancing over again, he didn't say anything either, but he was smirking as she drove.

The water was a blue so deep that it looked crystal. The surface was flat and smooth, and there were white bubbles on the water, stirred into the stillness by the motion of fish and the dipping of fish tails. A single seagull stood on the edge of a stone jetty, where a fisherman sat with his net, looking up at the sun-soaked sky. As Lily revved up the engine and turned the boat, she was reminded of so many days back in Aruba. So many days she'd spend boating with her father—and with Kara.

The dream she'd had earlier snuck back into her mind. It had freaked her the hell out. Why had she been having such disturbing dreams about Kara lately? It had been years since her sister went missing, and yet clearly, Lily's subconscious was trying to tell her something.

She didn't have time to think about what that was right now. She had to focus on the case, and she would—but in these moments, when she had a second to breathe, she really couldn't help but remember her past.

Stay focused, Lily.

Eagle Eye was only a ten-minute boat ride out, and Lily had the coordinates up on her phone. Lily was quiet as she drove, but unfortunately for her, Xander had other plans. "I hope your boyfriend doesn't think too badly of me for stealing his girl for a few hours."

Lily glanced at him. She didn't have a boyfriend—not anymore—but she wasn't about to take the bait from Xander. "If he's anything like you, he probably doesn't have any problem moving on."

Xander chuckled. "Well, that's good. You can't have a problem moving on when you don't even have a boyfriend, right?"

Her jaw tightened. What was his game here? "You knew I was single, so why did you bring up my boyfriend?"

"I didn't know," Xander said. "I guessed based on your reaction. Now I know. Guess that's one thing I do have in common with you—we both have a hard time getting attached."

Lily noticed the way he said it—so nonchalant, so casual—and she couldn't help but scoff. "A hard time? Yes, I'm sure that's what you'd call it. Now, can you shut up and focus on the case?"

Xander laughed. "Aye-aye, Captain."

At long last, the island appeared ahead. Lily couldn't get there faster, working with Xander was proving to be a complete pain in the ass. But they were here now.

Lily slowed down and scanned the horizon. It was just as she'd guessed: the body of water around the island was littered with janky-looking boats, and there was even a small flotilla of fishing boats keeping their distance but throwing out lines.

The sinking feeling returned to her belly—there were so many people here. They'd be lucky if they could pinpoint anybody in particular.

She turned to Xander and said as much. "This isn't going to be easy," she said. "There's at least fifty boats out on the water, not to mention all the seagull shit."

And as Lily got closer, she noticed a group of islanders off to the side.

They were carrying guns.

Shit.

Xander saw it too. He straightened up beside her, allowing his persona to drop into something more serious. "Looks like we should've brought backup."

Lily swallowed. "Keep your cool, Agent Jackson. We aren't in the US. You might not be used to boys like them—the worst thing you can do is come across as threatening. They're holding guns, but they won't use them unless we make them feel like they have to."

"You sound pretty damn confident about that," Xander said.

Lily swallowed, hard. She wasn't completely confident, but she also wasn't going to back away.

"Let's pose as customers, say we're here to buy some boat parts," she said. The police boat they'd taken was an undercover, so they wouldn't immediately scream that they were with law enforcement. "Don't take out your badge, okay?" Lily said. "Play it cool."

Xander nodded, although Lily could sense his unease. "I'm following your lead on this one then, Dawn. Sounds like you know how to handle these island boys. I might lose my temper a little if I get a gun shoved in my face."

"That's the last thing we want. Just follow my lead." As much as it made Lily's skin crawl, there was one plan of action that would work best here. "We're pretending to be a couple from this moment on, got it?"

Xander let out a stiff laugh. "Must be my lucky day."

Lily bit back a harsh response as she killed the engine. They were close to the island, and the last thing she wanted was for people to see them fighting on board.

Lily glared. "Keep your voice down. And if they see us as a couple, they won't suspect anything—it's a way out of this situation that doesn't put anybody in any danger."

"Well, actually, it puts you in danger," Xander said. "And if I'm being their link to you, that puts me in danger too." With some more revving, Lily shot over towards the small fleet of boats—no more than flat-bottomed skiffs with run-down engines attached to them.

She slowed down and brought the boat around. She hated whenever people got on her nerves; now she had to pretend she was in love with Xander? It was the opposite of appealing, but whatever got the job done would be good.

"Pull up, beside that fishing boat," Xander said. He pointed towards the deck of a wooden boat with two men on it and what looked like Walleye caught in a net. Lily noticed one of the men had a gun tucked in his belt.

Lily wasn't sure if they'd seen her or him, but they were staring straight ahead, looking like they didn't have anything to hide.

Her heart was pounding fast as she pulled the boat even with them. They didn't say anything for a moment—they were looking at her and then Xander, staring curiously at them. Then, Lily waved.

"Hi there," she said, smiling and putting her hands on her hips. She let Xander moor the boat to the dock. "We're here to buy some parts."

The man with the gun simply nodded, not fazed. They were off to a good start. Lily got off the boat, landing on the dock, and saw there was a pathway that led up to a shack. There were various people milling about—mostly unarmed, mostly looking like ordinary islanders. It didn't seem like anyone lived here, though. The island was so small, and the only structure Lily could see was the shop and some fishing shacks down the coastline.

Xander was clearly uneasy, his expression tight as he looked around the island, catching eyes with some people—notably, the men with guns.

"Come on, honey," Lily said through gritted teeth.

Xander followed behind her, and they headed up the path toward the shop.

The islanders started to notice them, clearly agitated by Xander's presence. Some of them went back to their fishing. Some of them didn't. Lily felt Xander's hand on her lower back as they headed up the path. "We should try and get rid of some of these," he said, glaring at a few men who looked like trouble.

And then there was that man.

Lily heard Xander suck in a breath beside her. One of the islanders—a big man—had stood up, heading for the path with big, angry steps. The island was small—there were no secrets here—and maybe he could smell that Lily and Xander were not exactly friends.

Still. Lily wasn't here to cause any trouble. She just wanted answers on that missing part.

So, she acted as though everything were fine and continued on her way to the shop. To add some extra flair, she looped her arm through Xander's so they seemed more believable, even though holding him like that definitely made her skin crawl.

Lily stole a glance over her shoulder. The islanders who'd noticed them seemed to have gone back to their business. She let out a breath as they walked up to the shop and went inside.

The boat shop was a mess. Tools were lying on the ground, and there were various boxes open and half-full of random bits. There was a small desk in the back corner, but it probably wasn't used often.

"Welcome," a voice said from the back, and then an old man emerged from behind the counter, wiping his hands on his apron and walking slowly over to them. It was dark in the shop, but a bit of light seeped in through the windows and emanated off the single bulb on the ceiling. "I'm guessing you're here to buy some parts?"

"Yes, sir," Lily explained. She kept her tone polite, her posture dutiful—and kept the tight grip on Xander's arm. "I'm very sorry to bother you."

Lily tried not to be paranoid, but she couldn't help but feel watched. The shopkeeper walked slowly over to them near the front of the store. He turned towards Xander, who hadn't flinched or shifted.

"What are ya lookin' for?" he asked. He had tanned skin and a bald head with thick lines on his face and a scar down his eye. He had clearly lived a long—and rough—life.

Lily pulled up the photo of the missing part's twin piece and showed the man. "I lost the other one," Lily said, "so I'm looking for a piece just like this."

The man narrowed his eyes at it. "Ya know . . . it's so odd . . . someone just brought one of these things in." He looked up and down Xander. "Where are you from again?"

Lily swallowed. He was clearly suspicious.

"I was born here on the islands, but my husband here is from America."

The man looked at Xander, who tipped his head and said, "Howdy."

Lily looked over her shoulder. They were the only ones in the store. The plan had been to stay under cover, but if this guy could remember who brought in the part, it could change everything.

Lily had to risk it.

She shot Xander a look, and he nodded back.

"Actually, sir," Lily said, taking out her badge and flashing it. "We're with the FBI."

The man's eyes narrowed. "What the hell is this about?"

"We're trying to find the person who may have sold you that boat part," Lily said.

The old man scowled. "Why should I help you?"

Lily let out a breath. The two of them were alone in the store. If he decided to quit talking and leave, they were up shit creek without a paddle.

There were several ways they could tackle it.

One: they could threaten him with the force of the FBI, the police, et cetera. Lily didn't see that ending well, considering this guy had armed friends on the island, and Lily and Xander were on their own.

Two: Lily could tell him the truth, that there were three girls dead now, and try to prey upon his humanity. He was grizzled and rough, but even men like him had daughters and wives. Maybe he would care.

She wasn't sure which was going to work. It was risky, but maybe if they could get him on their side, it wouldn't be all bad.

Ultimately, number two had to be the winner. She had to trust him and hope for the best.

“We’re investigating the murder of three different girls,” Lily said.

“The guy’s a murderer,” Xander interjected suddenly. He gave a grunt-like sigh as he looked at the floor.

The old man’s brows shot up. He focused on Lily. “Is this true?”

“The part I just showed you was missing from a victim’s boat,” Lily said. “If you have it here, and you know who brought it in, it could be immensely helpful. Three innocent women are dead, and we only want to find out what happened to them.”

The old man frowned, his face wrinkling. He was silent for a moment. Lily didn’t have time for silence. It was a gamble, an audacious move because if her instincts on the guy were wrong, then she and Xander were shit out of luck.

“I . . . did hear about some tourists who had been found dead,” the man eventually said. He sighed. “The man who brought the part in—I don’t care for him anyway. He is a thug. If you really think he could be involved, then I won’t protect him.”

Lily’s heart jumped. “What is his name?”

“Paul Hanna,” the man said. “I don’t know much about him, but he often comes in here and bullies me into paying more for his parts than what they’re worth. I didn’t want to buy this one, since it was missing its other half, but . . .” He went over to a shelf and picked up a part, bringing it over. He handed it to Lily.

It was the exact missing piece from Megan’s boat.

“I don’t know where he lives,” the man said. “Really, this is all I can tell you.”

“We’ll figure that out.” Lily looked at Xander, then back at the man. “Thank you for this.”

He nodded, his face grim. “Now, I really suggest you get off this island before anyone else realizes who you are.”

Lily didn’t need to be told twice. They had what they needed.

Paul Hanna’s fingerprints were all over this. And he had a lot to answer for.

CHAPTER EIGHTEEN

Out on the open seas, Lily maneuvered the boat back toward Freeport's coast. The mid-morning sun blazed like a giant, incandescent ball of fire in the sky, hanging right in the middle. Rays of light spilled over the water's surface and up onto their faces, giving them warmth and life. It was all beautiful here, but no amount of beauty could shake the nerves in Lily's gut as they soared toward Paul Hanna's last known address.

Xander sat back in the boat, on his phone, reading up as much as he could on the guy through their database. They had his address—now all they needed was him.

"Damn," Xander said, his voice carrying over the sound of the engine. Lily looked back.

"Guess this guy's known for stealing parts from tourists and selling them," he said. "He's got himself a nice little reputation. Even more than that—there are some rumors that he's dipping his feet into human trafficking."

Lily's gut twisted.

Human trafficking.

It still blew her mind that something like that could happen here, in such a beautiful place. There were people enslaved by monsters everywhere, but there were people here who were buying them.

No—she couldn't go there. Not now. She needed to focus on the task ahead of her. This was a serious matter, and she couldn't go chasing rabbits when she needed to stay focused and plug this leak in the dam.

But she couldn't ignore it because if Paul Hanna was involved in this trafficking, then what did that mean for their case? Why would he switch from stealing boat parts to human trafficking to murder? The first two, he clearly got something out of it, but why murder?

"Real piece of work," Xander said, shutting off his phone. Lily felt the boat rock as he stood up and made his way to the front, standing beside her. She shot him a look.

"What?"

"Relax, I'm just stretching my legs." He let out a sigh. "Why are you always so high-strung, anyway?"

Lily shook her head and laughed. "Funny thing is, Jackson, I'm not high-strung. You just have a really good way of getting under my skin."

"Must be the Southern thing," he said. "I've made an effort to stop calling you sweetheart. Believe it or not, I'm not this crazy asshole."

"I never said you were a crazy asshole. I just find you a little too cavalier given how serious these circumstances are."

"I ain't cavalier, Dawn. I'm serious when I need to be. I even let you take the lead back there on that island, even though I'm way older than you."

Lily kept her hands on the wheel but looked up at Xander. He'd taken off his sunglasses and stared down at her with intense green eyes.

"That's another thing that pisses me off," she said. "You keep bringing up your age as if you have forty years on me. You only have seven. My last partner is retired now, so I've dealt with experienced agents before—none of them have been nearly as cocky as you."

"Not cocky," Xander said quietly. "Just determined. It's called confidence, sugar."

"You do realize that confidence actually comes with experience, right? I'm gaining experience—you're probably losing it." She said the last bit with a grin. For once, the banter was amusing her more than it was annoying her.

And Xander could take the joke, because he said, "Thank you for the compliment."

They both laughed.

"There," he said suddenly, and Lily frowned at him.

"What?"

"I get to see your more relaxed side."

Lily shook her head, focusing on the sea in front of her. "Let's just focus on the case. Please." The two of them were alone now, just her and Xander, alone with this new information in such a way that they had to be careful how they handled it. "Finding out how Hanna's involved in this is our first step."

"So let's try to find him," Xander said. "I figure he's still on the island, but who knows? Maybe he's got some other boat he's using to hide out on. We should hit up his house first."

Lily nodded, pointing their boat further along the coast. They needed luck on their side—Paul Hanna was bound to be wary of people digging into his life now. He lived just up the coast, and his house was only a short walk up the beach, according to the GPS.

The boat flew over the surface of the ocean. Lily kept an eye out as they approached the shore, then slowed when they got close, pulling into a little dock. She dropped anchor and hopped off the boat, hitting the wet sand below her.

A group of seagulls swooped down around her, squawking and flapping their wings.

Xander hopped off after her, and they both walked up the beach.

The house wasn't quite beachfront. It was about a block away to the edge of the forest and the furthest possible point from the water, where the sand was marked by roads, lost children's toys, and puddles of mud. Paul Hanna didn't seem to spend much time outside—already, they could tell that much. And his home didn't offer any secrets. It was pretty small, likely little more than a hovel really. They walked up the footpath and across the surrounding lawns. Lily noticed a shed near the back of the property. The rest of the place was sort of a dump: garbage bags out front, broken flowerpots, and cigarette butts everywhere. They reached the rickety front door and knocked.

No answer.

"Been a while since anyone's been here," Xander said.

Lily rang the bell and stepped back, waiting.

No answer. There was no way no one was home—a car was parked just inside the garage, barely hidden from view. Still . . . nothing.

Lily pressed her ear against the door. She could hear sounds, footsteps, but they were on the other side of the house.

Xander shouldered her aside and looked through the front window. He motioned to her, then back at her ear, indicating she should try again. Still nothing.

That same instinct that had kept her alive so far told her not to break in—not yet at least. Not without backup anyway.

"We'll check out the back," she said to Xander, who nodded.

"Sneaky bastard might be trying to sneak out," he said.

Then, Lily heard a loud thump. She froze.

"What—" Xander started, but Lily held up her hand.

Another thump. This time, from above.

"He's on the roof," she said.

More thumps and bangs from above them.

Shit.

They ran quickly back around the house, where the roof jutted just out of view over the edge of the trees. As they rounded it, Lily looked up at the chimney—only to see a man stuffing something inside of it.

What the hell?

"Hey!" Lily shouted.

The man—Paul Hanna—looked down at them in shock. He was a short, stocky man with black hair and a mustache, and as soon as he saw them, he reached for something.

Lily knew that motion.

She dove to the side, tackling Xander down with her, as a loud gunshot resonated through the air.

Lily ducked for cover with Xander, and they both pulled out their guns. *Bastard!* Paul Hanna fired another shot randomly, and it penetrated the earth beside them, sending bits of dirt and grass into the air.

Now what?

"You two!" Paul shouted, not answering. "Get back!" He fired another shot at them, but he was a bad shot. Lily crouched behind an old oak tree, her gun pointed upward. Xander was already crouching behind another tree across from her. They needed to use that to their advantage, and Xander was thinking the same thing.

They pointed their guns at the roof and shot. The sound resonated through the air, and through the chaos, Lily thought she heard something.

A woman screaming.

What the—?

She looked in the direction of the sound. It sounded like it came from . . .

The shed?

Paul Hanna fired off another shot, cutting her thoughts short.

"Up there!" Lily shouted, aiming up at the roof. She could hear Hanna's footsteps pounding along the roof as he tried to escape, and she barked, "Xander, look out! He's trying to get away!"

"I got 'im," Xander said, eyes steely. "You go."

He'd heard the woman screaming too.

Xander dashed away to the other side of the house, and Lily ducked behind another tree. With her gun still out, she checked all around the backyard to ensure she wouldn't be shot as she crossed to the shed.

She looked out across the lawn to check that the coast was clear, then sprinted across until she hit the shed door. It was huge, about ten feet tall and three feet wide, with a little window at the top. Lily ripped open the door. It was dark, except for a little light from small holes that let light in from above her head. She peered inside—and staring back at her was a woman with a gag in her mouth, her hands and legs tied.

Lily's heart dropped. She dove into the shed and quickly untied the woman, ripping off her gag. The woman began speaking to her in Spanish:

"¡Ayúdame! ¡Me tomó! ¡Me secuestró!" *Help me! He took me! He kidnapped me!*

Lily gently grabbed the woman's arms. She was young, maybe twenty, and had black hair, tanned skin, and dark eyes. Apparently, she didn't speak a word of English.

"Estas segura ahora," Lily said in Spanish. *You're safe now.*

The woman cried and gasped, grabbing onto Lily and holding her.

"Lo siento, perdóname por favor," Lily said. "No te preocupes. Te liberaré." *I'm sorry, I apologize, please don't worry. I'll set you free.*

Lily's Spanish was a little rusty, but it was good to have knowledge of another language. She was just glad that she and her father had been so open to learning it while she was a child. She heard screams from outside and grabbed the woman's hands again.

"Seguro," Lily said, trying to sound gentle. "Tranquila." *Safe. Calm down.*

But Lily couldn't calm down yet. She had to have Xander's back. He was still chasing after Paul Hanna, who was armed.

Lily wasn't Xander's biggest fan, but like hell would she let him get shot. He was still her partner. And Lily was nothing if not loyal.

She ran out of the shed, going in the direction she'd seen Xander take off in.

Holding her gun out and ready, Lily peered into the trees, trying to find her partner.

Any sound she heard, any movement, she turned around to face it.

There! She spotted him and Hanna in the distance, sprinting through the trees. Xander got a good way ahead of her, and Paul Hanna turned to shoot at him, but Xander dove out of the way just in time. He got back up and charged after Paul yet again, and this time, he managed to tackle him. They fell to the ground and rolled down a slope into a ditch.

Lily ran after them, her feet pounding against moist grass. But as soon as she reached the edge of the ditch, she stopped, skidding on her heels.

Xander had his gun pointed on Paul Hanna, who held his hands up in surrender. Lily watched as Xander twisted Paul's hands behind his back and slapped cuffs on him. Then, he looked up at Lily, holding his prize.

"Told you I get results," he said.

Lily let out a breath, relieved.

They got him.

CHAPTER NINETEEN

Lily faced down Paul Hanna in the Freeport interrogation room, disgust curling inside her at the way this man's eyes stared into her soul. He wasn't talking, even as Xander barked questions at him.

"Give it up, jackass," Xander said. "We've got you. So, the sooner you start answering our questions, the sooner we can all get the hell out of here."

Paul didn't budge.

There was only one thing Lily was grateful for—the woman who'd been trapped in Paul's shed was now free, and she would be returned to her family. She claimed to be from Cuba and was vacationing here when Paul snatched her from her tour group. She had only been taken that day, which was why her disappearance hadn't landed on the police's radar.

According to the girl, Paul hadn't said much about what he'd planned to do with her, but they could only assume the worst: that the rumors of Paul getting into human trafficking were true.

But if that were the case, then why did he kill Sophia Harris, Marie Levesque, and Megan Frost? They were all American tourists, so for him to switch to a Cuban tourist was a bit of a change in MO. Still, Paul Hanna had his fingerprints all over this case, and Lily could only assume that he was guilty.

Xander's bulldog approach wasn't getting anywhere, so Lily took over. On the way to the precinct, she'd taken some time to get to know Paul Hanna's file: he was born here in Freeport but was in and out of foster care; he had a history of criminal activity and had very little money.

"Paul," she said, starting slow. Paul's near-black eyes landed on hers, but Lily could see the indignation in them. "You're not a bad guy, Paul—you're just doing what you have to in order to survive, right? That's why you stole the boat parts. That's why you started trafficking girls."

Paul stayed silent and looked away.

Lily sighed.

"You see, I was a street kid once," she said, leaning against the table so that her face was close to his. "I would have done anything to make sure my little sister and I could have food, clean water, and a place to sleep." She kept talking as she locked eyes with him. "So, you know . . . I get it. I don't blame you for any of this."

It was a bit of truth embellishment, of course—Lily and Kara had a good life with their parents, and they always had food. But what was true in it was how much Lily would have fought for her sister.

She saw the corner of Paul's mouth turn up in a grin before he collected himself and straightened his lips again to say, "Váyanse, pendejas. I didn't start trafficking girls," he said, and for a moment, Lily was taken aback by how strongly he said the words. *Go away, assholes.*

But then . . . he did start trafficking girls. Paul just hadn't come out and admitted it yet. "You don't have to be afraid to tell us," Lily said, watching him closely. "We already know the truth, Paul, so denying it will get you nowhere."

Paul was quiet, looking away.

"We just want to help you," Lily said, anxious to get him to trust them a little bit more so they could get to the bottom of this whole thing. Maybe there were more girls like the Cuban woman who were trapped somewhere right now. If there were more captives, Lily had to rescue them as soon as possible. "Are there any more girls, Paul? The police are already raiding your home, so if you have anything else you want to confess to, now is the time."

Beside Lily, Xander crossed his arms and gave a tiny scoff that only she would pick up on. She shot him a glare—she could tell he didn't approve of her diplomatic method, but right now it was working a hell of a lot better than his. At least Lily got him to talk.

She refocused on Paul. "Tell us, Paul, and maybe we can go easier on you. You've already had such a hard life."

That perked his interest. "How could you possibly go any easier on me?" he asked, and Lily was happy to see that he was at least still listening. She thought of Xander's gun being close to Paul's head, and she knew it would only be a matter of time before her partner lost his temper.

"Maybe we could make sure you get better food—I bet the food in prison isn't very good, is it?"

Paul shrugged.

"Maybe we could even get you some books," Lily said. "Books can be very good for a guy like you." She watched him carefully to see if her words were getting to him. "But all I want is for you to tell me the truth."

She watched Paul carefully, analyzing every twitch of a muscle or line in his face, but there seemed to be no real change of emotion from him as he stared at the table between them.

Lily knew that homelessness and youth without stable homes was a risk factor for becoming involved in criminal activity, so she tried to sympathize with him, to put herself in his shoes and relate to him. "If I had had a chance, I would have escaped from my life too. I would have done anything to make sure my family would be taken care of."

"Yes!" Paul spat out. "But I didn't do nothin'. This shit is total bullshit!"

"How about we get back to the part about trafficking," Xander said, stepping forward. "We have all your ring recorded, you know. We have proof."

Paul flopped back into his chair. "Oh yeah?" he yelled. "Where are those girls now? They takin' the fall for this shit? No! They're free as goddamn birds! Fuck this shit!"

His temper flared, and he started hitting the table with his cuffed fists. "It's not my goddamn fault some dumb mutts called the cops!"

"I don't know what you're thinking, asshole," Xander said, leaning toward him until Paul closed his eyes at the sight of another looming figure. "But whatever it is, you're wrong. You're going to be behind bars for a long time, so why don't you fess up, huh? We've got you on the trafficking. So, let's talk about the murders."

"What fuckin' murders!?" Paul exclaimed. "I didn't—I never killed anyone!"

Lily wasn't buying it. With a sigh, she took out three photos, all of the victims when they were alive. She slid them across the table, looking at Paul's face, gauging his reactions.

"These girls," Lily said. "You know them, don't you, Paul?"

"What? Hell no!"

"Sure you don't." Xander shook his head. "Seems familiar with them, though, doesn't it?"

"I don't know anything about these damn women," Paul spit out.

And then he seemed to see them for the first time. He looked from the photos to Lily, and she saw that his eyes had opened in fear with what he realized was happening. "You're pinning this shit on me?" he demanded. "That's bullshit—I haven't killed a single person, ever!"

Lily pulled out the boat piece and dropped it on the table. Paul looked at it and squinted. "What is this?"

"You recognize it, Paul," Lily said. "You sold this part, didn't you? You stole it when you killed this woman." She pointed to the photo of Megan.

He looked closer at the photo. "Wait—that's her?" He met Lily's eyes, this time, pleading. "Look, I did break into that chick's boat and I was trying to steal parts, but then I saw someone coming up the dock, and I ran for it. It was her—maybe, I don't know, she had sunglasses on. But she was alive, I'm telling you. I didn't kill these women," Paul repeated. "I don't know who the hell did."

Lily's heart dropped. There was a sinking feeling in her gut that they were wrong about him being guilty, but they had no hard evidence pointing to anyone else.

"You're lying," Xander said. "Why else would you be so scared?"

"Because you guys say that I killed people! I'm not used to talking to the fucking cops, asshole!" Paul spat at him. "Leave me alone! I wanna go home!"

Xander pushed back his chair with a loud scrape and crossed his arms, staring down at Paul with a dark look on his face.

Lily looked at her partner sadly and realized what was happening. He was so adamant about his theory, it hadn't occurred to him that he might be wrong.

She slid the photo of Megan back over to Paul and readdressed him. "Did she say anything when you saw her, Paul? Tell me everything you remember." As she listened, Lily began to doubt herself. Maybe Paul really wasn't their killer. Maybe their search would go on longer than they had thought.

"Come on, Paul," Xander said with a chuckle. "Spill it!"

A stricken look came over Paul's face as he glanced from the boat part to the photos still lying on the table. He swallowed hard and furrowed his brow with effort as the words got stuck in his throat. "I . . . I just ran away, she didn't say shit!"

"And when was this?" Lily asked.

"Four freakin' days ago! I've been out of town for the past few days, I just got back this morning, and then I saw that girl with her tour group and I just—" He took a breath. "I just took her, okay? It's the first time I've done it. I thought, with the right buyer, I could make big bucks off her, but I'm not a trafficker and I'm definitely not a killer. I'm just trying to get a better life, man."

"At the expense of someone else's?" Lily's nostrils flared. The thought was disgusting.

But as much as that pissed her off, something in Paul's statement stood out.

He said he was out of town.

"Where were you?" Lily asked.

"I was in Butlock Harbor, at a hotel," he said.

"Really?" Lily lifted an eyebrow. "And why exactly were you there?"

Paul looked at her with his brows knit low as though he was trying to figure out what she was implying. "I was visiting a friend," he said slowly.

"Do you have an alibi for all of these murders? For every single one?" Lily asked him. *What if we're wrong about him?* she suddenly thought. She watched Paul closely, but if his panic returned, he hid it well.

"Call the hotel, man," he said. "I was there. So, if this chick died while I was gone, then you've got nothing on me for the murder."

Lily's eyes hardened on him. She hated the thought that they'd wasted more time on this guy, although whether Paul was the killer or not, he still belonged behind bars. The woman in his shed could testify for that.

Either way, they had to follow this up.

Lily stood up, and so did Xander. They both looked down on Paul as Lily said, "Get comfortable, Paul Hanna. We'll look into your alibi. But you're still going to prison."

"Fuck this!" Paul shouted. "Goddamn, what do you think you're doing!? You've been stalking me! I didn't do anything!"

Lily watched as he struggled against his handcuffs. She could see it in his eyes—he knew he was screwed, and he wasn't going to accept it easily.

"Get the hell out of here, you goddamn lunatics," he said. His eyes darted back and forth frantically, looking for a way out. "I've never killed anyone! I'm not going to jail!"

Lily watched him. The vein on his forehead looked like it was going to burst, through Lily could swear she saw hope in the set of his jaw and shoulders.

With an incongruous laugh, he held up his cuffed hands and shook his head. “Go arrest someone else,” he said. “You’re mistaken. I’m not your killer. You’re totally wrong.”

Xander scoffed at him, but both Lily and her partner left the room before they did any lasting damage.

A couple of phone calls, and they’d find out the truth.

CHAPTER TWENTY

Whenever the sun was out, he wished to see the stars, but he had to admit, the light of day gave him ample room to see who his next pick would be. As he floated on his boat like a buoy at sea, he peered through his binoculars at the cruise ship on the horizon, coming toward the Grand Bahama Island.

And what a magnificent vessel that cruise ship was. The ship was an oasis on the horizon, with the deck a white gold that turned the sea the color of opals. Its railings were a beautiful lattice of silver and platinum. It was like a jewel box on its way to an engagement.

He knew the real jewels were the passengers inside.

"Alright, let's see who we have," he said aloud to no one, his back to the blue sky. "Bob's a baker, Stan's a butcher, Pete's a professor, and Brian's been shot—that's enough for now . . . I'll see you tonight, children."

He scanned the deck of the boat, zeroing in on the many young people aboard.

After all, they were the best kind of people to watch.

But it wasn't only age that he favored. He could choose youth, but wizened experience was just as good sometimes. Either way, it was good to have someone who could talk back.

It was Sunday afternoon, beautiful weather and idyllic conditions for a day on the open sea.

Everyone aboard had a smile on his or her face, and there was an excitement in the air, an excitement so palpable it was impossible not to infect everyone within ten feet. For a moment, he imagined himself, young and infallible, atop that ship with them. What a life . . .

But no, he couldn't afford to dream. He needed to find a girl. A beautiful, brown-haired girl.

He found her on the deck that night.

Her hair was brown and fell in pretty curls about her shoulders, their bounce keeping time with the music she danced to. For a moment, he wondered if she was Her—but no, those eyes were green, where Hers were a shade of blue that he'd never seen in person.

However, the second girl caught his attention as well.

She was older than the first girl, perhaps nineteen or twenty years old, and sturdier, too, with a confident walk that exuded strength and vibrancy. She moved through her day with a smile. Her skin glowed warm in the Caribbean sun.

She had stars in her eyes, literally. Bright eyes that contrasted with raven hair and dark skin. But best of all was the way she carried herself; she had a regal air about her as if she ruled this ship. She didn't need to dance in the open air to have fun.

"Yes," he said, "very pretty."

He kept his eyes on his work, smiling.

A slender brunette stood at the railing, basking in the sun, as if she'd been plucked from an Italian painting of the Renaissance. She was wearing a white dress that dazzled against the water surrounding it like a fishbowl. Her hair was done up in an elegant bun, making her look like someone's muse—a Victorian-era beauty with yards of curls and an exquisite stare. But the more he studied her features, the more he realized she was no younger than twenty-five or twenty-six. A bit too old to become one of his stars; he liked them a bit younger, to capture the essence of forever youth. Only the brightest could become one of his stars, so bright they would help guide Janie back home to him.

Once he had made his selection, he would find them on the ship and lure them away.

He loved to pick the youngest, the loneliest, the ones who were a little lost.

The ones whose eyes shone like the moon, who made their home in the starlight.

He didn't truly harm any of his Stars, but he did need to find a way on that boat. He needed to find a way to get them to take a few steps out of the sunlight. He could whisper words into their ears about being less lonely, about being happier and living for decades otherwise unseen.

He'd get the right words in their ear, even if he had to take them somewhere else. It was the sort of thing that he'd worked very hard on over time. Luring someone away from something was an art form, one he'd honed to perfection over the years. And once he found his stars, they were happy forever afterward. Happy because they truly believed they belonged up there with the stars. They never tired of seeing the sun rise and set.

Those were the ones who would shine the brightest in their celestial homes.

He sighed. "I can't wait to see you again, Janie."

Can't wait.

CHAPTER TWENTY ONE

Back at the house, Lily sat at the coffee table with her laptop open, and Megan Frost's file out.

Paul Hanna's alibi had checked out. On the days all three women went missing, he was confirmed to be on another island, too far to have caused their deaths.

It was a dead end.

As much as that frustrated Lily, she was thankful to have saved the Cuban woman, and any other women who Paul might have decided to attack down the line. Women weren't products, like boat parts, he could just steal and sell on the black market, and Lily was grateful she'd put an end to that.

Even still. That left her with her head in the sand, having no names to pursue now.

But she did have more information on Megan Frost now.

Megan was twenty-one years old, and she had travelled alone to the Bahamas with the intention of writing a book.

She was in the middle of a rough patch in life and needed to get away. As the daughter of a rich CEO of a tech company back in Florida, she had her own yacht here in Freeport. She'd taken a flight over, received her yacht from the yacht club, then relaxed in her island paradise—until her unfortunate end.

Megan had never reported the boat part going missing. Perhaps she just didn't want to bother herself with it. But since Paul Hanna was cleared, Lily knew that she couldn't focus on that anymore. She had to look elsewhere.

Moving away from the details of Megan herself, she pulled up the photos the coroner had sent of Megan's body. There she was: pale-skinned with dark hair. The image made Lily's heart drop.

The official cause of death for all three girls was drowning.

Lily looked closer at the image of Megan's face and neck. There were the ligature marks . . .

She went back to the photo of Marie's body. She, also, had slight ligature marks. Sophia didn't appear to have any, but still, it seemed significant.

The coroner report said their tracheas were undamaged, so strangling was not the cause of death. So, what were these marks?

Lily leaned back on the couch as the door to the house opened, and Xander walked in carrying two coffees. Lily shot him a look.

"You didn't have to do that," she said. She'd thought he was just talking to the local police. He walked over and handed her a warm cup, which she accepted. She could use the boost.

"Consider it an apology," he muttered, sitting on the couch next to her, a good distance away. "I know I've been pissing you off, and we've been getting off on the wrong foot. I say let bygones be bygones and start fresh."

"That doesn't sound like you," she said. What was with the change of character?

Xander laughed. "You've been handling this case like a pro, Dawn. I shouldn't have doubted you."

Lily wasn't good at compliments, even if she did feel like Xander was unnecessarily condescending toward her before. "Thanks, Jackson," she said. "I do my best."

"It's just—I'm used to being in charge," he said. "And I'm gunning for Special Agent. I feel like solving this case could be huge for my career, so if I've been too Gung-ho, that's why."

She leaned back, taking a sip of the coffee. It ignited her senses. "So why apologize now?"

He shrugged. "I just want to get this thing solved and work together as efficiently as possible."

Xander glanced at her. "I've never been too much of a giver when it comes to thank you's."

She laughed. "Maybe that would change if you got more compliments then."

"Maybe." He leaned back on the couch. "The moment we find any names or potential suspects, we're golden. I think we can solve this thing. Be a good duo. FBI wouldn't pair us together for nothin'."

Lily nodded. That was true. She did wonder why the FBI chose them to be together.

"What division are you from?" Lily asked.

"South Florida," he said. "And you're from Quantico."

"They must've paired us for a reason," Lily said.

"Yeah." He laughed. "I'm the aggressor, and you're the diplomat."

"And this works?" Lily asked. "Two agents who can't stand each other trying to solve the case together?"

He smirked. "Maybe we have something else in common. Did you ever think of that?"

"I have," Lily teased back, sipping her coffee and leaning forward on the couch. "Anyway, did you learn anything while you were out?"

He nodded. "The police are taking care of Paul Hanna." He took a sip from his coffee. "You?"

"Yes." She leaned forward in anticipation, taking a deep breath before blurting out what she thought about Megan Frost and the marks around her throat. "There appears to be ligature marks on Megan's neck, and Marie's. Their cause of deaths were drowning, not strangulation, so what is with the marks?"

She thought on it for a moment. Something about the statement from the coast guard earlier stood out.

Cut her free.

"He said they cut her free," Lily said. "Do you remember that?"

"I do," Xander said. "In the chaos, we never followed up."

"Was she tied up?" Eagerly, Lily took out her phone and dialed Officer Chandler of the coast guard. Within a few rings, he picked up.

"This is Chandler."

"Officer Chandler, it's Lily Dawn of the FBI," she said. "I'll make this quick—you said earlier Megan was 'cut free.' What did you mean by that?"

"We told you, didn't we?" he said. "Ms. Frost was tied to the boat by a rope, and we cut her free upon arrival because we thought maybe we could save her. Looking back on it, we shouldn't have tampered with the scene, but—"

"It was around her neck?" Lily interrupted.

"Yes," he said. "We saw it and cut her free, but she was already too far gone."

Shit. This could change everything.

"Thank you, Officer Chandler," Lily said, hanging up the phone. She faced Xander, who had the same determined look on this face. Lily went on her laptop and checked the files. No rope was ever mentioned, and both Marie and Sophia were found floating aimlessly in the water. But Marie had the marks . . .

"Maybe Marie's rope came loose," Lily said.

"Maybe Sophia was tied up too," Xander said.

Feeling a rush of inspiration, Lily stood up and paced across the living room. The midday sun poured in through the open bay windows, giving them a great view of the ocean.

"Why were these girls tied up?" Lily said aloud.

"I don't know," Xander said. "Maybe the bastard dragged them through the water."

"They would have more obvious trauma if that were the case," Lily said. "The trauma is light."

All of this felt significant. And Lily wasn't sure where to go next. What did it all mean? Lily's head was spinning.

"I need some fresh air," she said, and she went toward the back door, stepping onto the back deck of the house. She breathed in the ocean air and leaned against the railing, staring out at the sea as waves lapped against the shore.

As much as Lily appreciated that Xander wanted to put effort in for their team, she couldn't help but think of her old partner, Special Agent Foster, who had retired not that long ago. Lily had been cycling through partners ever since.

Special Agent Foster was a tough nut to crack. A grizzled old man from the moment she'd met him.

Special Agent Foster had been the master of deduction. If Lily had ever had a partner who could complement her skills—it was him. As much as they argued and as hard as they worked at each other, Lily had loved working with him. Just thinking back on the days when he'd stood beside her made her feel a sense of longing so strong . . .

They had an interesting dynamic, though. There was something about working with Foster that made Lily feel safe—knowing a tough man like him had her back. And the fact that she didn't have to babysit him made it easier.

Foster wouldn't question her methods or decisions. He'd listen, and he'd give his input, no matter what. There was a kind of comfort in that. Was that what it was like to work with someone who truly respected you? In the whole time Foster was partnered with her, he never complained about anything she did, regardless of how many hours she put in or going above and beyond when it happened.

The man had retired, and Lily hadn't spoken to him in a couple of months. She didn't want to bother him; she knew he was living it up in

Mexico and wanted to put the FBI behind him. Still, Lily really needed his guidance at this moment.

She decided to risk it. She took out her phone and dialed his number.

He answered on the second ring.

"Hello?"

"Agent Seymour Foster," she said with a chuckle. "What do you think you're doing in Mexico?"

His chuckle came through the phone. "Agent Lily Dawn. I've been relaxing, and I haven't watched the news." He laughed. "I'm assuming I should be, if you're calling me."

Lily smiled slightly. "I know you're trying to put all this behind you, but I'd love to bounce this case off you, if you have time."

"Lily, I told ya before, you can call me anytime," Foster said.

Lily smiled, staring out at the sea before her. The truth was, Foster had been like a father to Lily for so many years. With her own parents not talking to her, she'd taken comfort in his guidance and mentorship.

"Thank you, Foster," Lily said. "I'm in the Bahamas—they transferred me over here to team up with the Caribbean government to find out what's going on. Three American tourists have been killed now, found floating out at sea."

"That won't be good for tourism," Foster said.

"Definitely not," Lily said. "Anyway, the cause of death for the three girls was drowning. However, I've noticed slight ligature marks around the necks of two of the bodies, and one girl was confirmed to have been left tied to her boat by the neck. However, that isn't what killed them."

For a moment, she could feel Foster thinking in silence over the phone. He didn't rush his thoughts. He liked to mull things over, think things through logically before he gave his input.

"That is odd," he eventually said. "It's as though the killer wanted them to be found floating like that. The question is, why?"

"Exactly," Lily said. "What does it mean?"

"Well, what floats in the water and is bound by rope?" Foster asked.

Lily had a feeling that he already knew. But this was what Foster was good at: getting Lily to think for herself. This was always how it was with Foster: he'd get her thinking, suggest the right things to look for, but he wouldn't outright tell her what it was she should be looking for. It drove her crazy, but it helped foster that critical thinking side of hers.

"A buoy," she said. "They were found floating like buoys."

"That could be it," said Foster. "Now you need to find out what that could mean about your killer."

"I'm scared I won't be able to find it in time," Lily said quietly, afraid if she said it out loud, it would really happen. "An innocent girl died tonight."

"Don't let that scare you," Foster said. "You're doing everything you can. Stay focused. Don't let your fears distract you. You're a solid agent, Dawn. You know your worth."

His kind words warmed the pit of Lily's stomach. What she wouldn't give to have a partner like Foster again. He always knew just what to say just when she needed it.

"Thanks, Foster," Lily said. "This means a lot."

"No problem," he said. "Listen, I have to go—try not to involve yourself too much in this, as hard as that might be."

Foster hung up the phone, leaving Lily alone with just the sea and her thoughts. She tried to be optimistic about the case and focus her thoughts on what would come next.

If the women were left in the water like buoys, then another thought struck her. They hadn't thought about where the women were left, as it had seemed to be random.

But what if it wasn't?

What if there was a pattern?

She raced back inside to see Xander on his laptop, frowning over the screen as he reviewed files. He looked up when she hurried to her laptop and sat down, pulling up a map.

"What the hell happened to you?" Xander asked.

She took a breath. "What if there's a pattern? What if the women weren't left there randomly? What if the killer tried to tie them to once place intentionally?"

"Damn," Xander said. "Hell of an epiphany. Let's check it out."

The coast guard had marked down the spots in which the women were found, and Lily cross-referenced each spot with a map of the area.

Megan was for sure left in the right spot, as she hadn't drifted away. For Marie, she had to account for the space she'd drifted off after being likely released from a rope. Sophia was found floating in an inlet—she could have drifted in from elsewhere, but maybe that was where he'd wanted her to be found.

She marked a dot where Megan and Sophia were found, then circled the general area where Marie was found.

What she had were three random dots.

Lily's mind was racing. Could they be stars? They didn't make a pattern at all, at least not one her brain could complete.

Xander leaned beside her. "It doesn't look like anything," he said. "Just three dots."

"No," Lily said. "They're not dots. They're stars. And it is a pattern, Xander."

She looked him in the eyes.

"It's the beginnings of a constellation."

CHAPTER TWENTY TWO

"What does this even mean?" Lily asked, leaning over the laptop. "It's a killer's way of saying, 'I've made a constellation, and now I'm going to make stars.'"

"Sounds like the right kind of crazy mentality we're looking for," Xander said. "But what constellation is it?"

Lily pulled up a list of them and cross referenced the dots. She tried Orion first. It didn't line up.

Next was Taurus—an actual bull. Another strike against it.

She kept cross-referencing. Gemini turned out to be two people, but with her limited knowledge of the constellations, it was hard to figure out which person was connected to the dots she had marked down.

"Damn," Lily said. "We're missing something here. Do you know which constellation starts with three stars?"

Xander took the laptop and looked through the list. "Leo is a pretty prominent constellation. I mean, those three stars right there? They're hard to miss."

Lily looked over. Xander put his finger on the screen, slowly drawing closer until they matched up with the spots that they'd pinpointed.

"Maybe it's Leo," she said. "But the pattern isn't complete. He could be making anything." Lily sighed, her mind going over it again and again. She turned to Xander. "And we have no idea who this person is."

But they had something to work off now. Maybe they were looking for some sort of local astronomy fanatic, some person who was obsessed with stars and constellations. Lily went online to do some digging. Freeport wasn't a huge city—surely, there was someone here they could pin this on.

She began searching for observatories first. There wasn't one in Freeport at all, so that narrowed down that search. Maybe a museum with a constellation exhibit? That didn't seem to exist here, either. The Bahamas was not known for celestial exhibits—people came here to relax and drink on the beach under the sun, and they could see plenty of real stars outside at night.

That got Lily's mind turning. Real stars. They also had the clue about boats and sailing.

"What combined stars and sailing?" Lily asked, thinking out loud.

Xander was doing his own research on the couch beside her. "Back in the day, sailors would use the sky to get themselves around, y'know, follow the north star and all that jazz."

"True," Lily said. "They could use the stars like a map. A map . . ."

Lily went back online and did some digging. Maybe they were looking for a cartographer—someone who was also a sailor. Her search brought her to a university website here in Freeport, focused on a man named Professor George Pinder.

He was a history professor and a cartographer. One of the courses he taught, according to the website, was how ancient people used the stars to navigate the seas.

He owned a private boat, of course—he had to have known more than a thing or two about that. Lily remembered how the coast guard had said Megan's boat looked like it had been hit by another vessel.

"I think I found our guy," Lily said.

Xander was there beside her, reading the same information. "Wow—it's pretty weird that he teaches this stuff. Is he into astrology or something?"

"Maybe," Lily said. "Look at his picture."

The professor was a tall, fit man in his fifties with thick, dark hair and a well-trimmed beard. "He looks like a serial killer," Xander said, squinting.

"I know it sounds crazy," Lily said, biting her lip as she pounded out an email to the professor. "But this has to be our guy."

"Bingo," Lily said.

"How the hell did you find that?" Xander asked.

Lily looked up at him and smiled. "It's what I do, Xander—my mind always finds the right piece of info to close a case." She slammed her laptop shut and stood. "Come on, let's go visit this Pinder fellow."

*

With its stucco yellow walls and red roof, the university was nothing like the ones back in the US. The maroon building was large and had two stories, with a flat red roof that gathered the sunlight and reflected it down upon the paths. There was no campus—the building was at the edge of a residential neighborhood and stood between a convenience store and a karaoke bar. The grass that edged up against it was trampled flat and littered with Styrofoam cups, sweet wrappers, and cigarette butts. It was located on the edge of the city, so Lily wasn't surprised to see this wasn't the most popular educational institute in town.

Her palms grew sweaty with anticipation as she and Xander made their way inside. "If he's teaching a class, we'll just have to interrupt," Lily said.

"Oh, we'll be interrupting alright," Xander said.

The inside of the building was a lot more modern than the outside—with its clean lines, arcs, and sharp corners, it almost looked like it had been airlifted right out of a university in California. The desks were metal and bolted down to the floor, and the tables were made of glass with metal bases.

There was no art on the walls that she could see, save for a poster of an anniversary celebration hanging up beside the wall near the elevator. Lily stared at it as they walked past. It boasted that this school was ranked one of the best in the country, twenty years ago.

"I'm sure he'll be happy to cooperate," Xander said sarcastically.

A secretary with brown hair and a kind smile sat behind the long, brown mahogany desk. The office was small and dingy, with a dirty window right over the desk. "Can I help you?" she asked.

Lily flashed her badge. "FBI—we need to see Professor Pinder right away."

The secretary's face went pale. "Oh, I believe he's in a lecture . . ."

"Sorry," Lily said. "It's urgent."

The woman nodded. "Well, his lecture hall is down the hallway at the very end to the right," she said. "I hope everything is okay."

Xander flashed the woman a smile. "All good, ma'am, don't you worry."

The plea for help in her eyes said she was definitely going to be worrying.

She was quick to go back to her work.

Xander gave Lily a questioning look. "What do you think?" he asked.

Lily shrugged. "I have no idea." They walked down the hall towards Professor Pinder's lecture hall. "But I have a feeling we're about to know everything."

When they approached the lecture hall—which was a large, dusty, peach room with rows of chairs like a movie theatre—she heard Professor Pinder talking.

"This is one of the earliest examples of engraving on the planet," he said.

His voice boomed through the speakers on either side of the room. The students, who were barely over twenty years old in Lily's estimation, looked up towards the projector screen above them.

"It was found in France, but it also just might have been engraved here in Freeport!"

A murmur went through the class. "It would have been very expensive to engrave this map," Professor Pinder said. "The people who commissioned it must have been very wealthy to have something like that crafted."

Lily didn't have time to waste. Her and Xander made their way past the rows of students, and that was when the professor noticed them. He stopped and asked, "Can I help you?"

Students whispered around as Lily and Xander reached the front of the room. Lily went right up to him and said, "FBI, Professor Pinder. We need a word."

He frowned. "Now? I'm in a lecture."

"It's important," she said.

He gritted his teeth against the annoyance, but said, "Okay then." He faced his class and raised his voice. "Students, I'll be right back. Please stay in your seats."

Lily steered the sweating professor out into the hallway, where the class whispered with nervous speculation, and where a handful of students lined the walls, watching with interest.

They went into the empty hallway. With a wincing look on his face, Professor Pinder asked, "What's this all about?"

"As we mentioned, we're with the FBI," Lily said. "We're looking into a series of crimes here on the island, and we were wondering if you could take us to your boat." If they could see his boat, they might find damage consistent with the damage on Megan's boat.

"What—right now?" he asked, flabbergasted.

"Please," Lily said.

The professor groaned. "Alright, let me just tell my class that I'm leaving for the day."

Lily nodded. She could at least give him that. "Fine. But make it quick."

*

Lily, Xander, and the professor arrived at the dock. The boat was a gorgeous grand trawler with a large cabin behind it, varnished wood all over, and two engines at its bottom. Beads of sweat formed on the professor's forehead—he wasn't quite sure how to handle all this.

"I got her back," he said. "She had been stolen a few years ago—did you know? She's the pride and joy of my fleet!"

"So, you were sailing today?" Lily asked.

He nodded. "But that's not why you're here..." He eyed her with suspicion. "What exactly are you looking for?"

"Let us handle that," Xander said.

Lily hopped on the boat. She knew exactly what she was looking for: signs of a collision. Somebody smashed into Megan Frost's boat, and if this Pinder had signs of it, then they'd have reasonable cause to bring him in for questioning.

She looked all over the outside of the boat—the front end was intact and had been recently waxed. She went and searched the back end where she discovered a dent on the right side of the boat and a piece of cracked metal on the pavement—it was hard to see, but it looked like the same kind of silver metal used on Megan's boat.

Lily's pulse picked up. She glanced back at a clueless-looking Pinder, who nervously wrung his hands together. Lily's eyes hardened. Was this his way of writing his own map? Had he been so obsessed with the stars and the sea that he resorted to killing innocent women? The pathology didn't quite make sense yet, but Lily had what she needed: reasonable cause.

"You found something?" Xander said.

"I sure did," Lily said. "Can you arrest this guy, Xander?"

He nodded. "That I can do." He called out to Pinder once again, this time with his hand on his gun. "Professor? Keep your hands where I can see them."

Pinder scrambled to keep his hands up in the air. "What's going on? What are you doing?"

"You're coming down to the station with us."

"What!? Why!? This is outrageous!" He looked up the shore, where there were groups of people, tourists, and islanders alike. "Help!" he called out, waving his arms.

"Settle down," Xander said. "Or I'll put you under for the transport."

"Help, police!" he screamed out. His voice was frantic, and he looked like he was about to break down crying. "My brother is a police officer—you can't do this to me!"

Lily arched an eyebrow at him. It seemed like anxiety had taken over the man, but he was being very over the top. Just as Lily was ready to put him in cuffs, two men wearing police uniforms appeared, jogging over the grass down to the beach. Freeport police officers.

"What's going on here?" one cop said, a tall, broad-chested bald guy.

Lily and Xander flashed their badges. "FBI. We need to bring this man in for questioning in relation to the recent tourist murders."

"Murders!?" Pinder exclaimed. "I didn't kill anyone!"

The police officer faced Lily. "We know this man. He's not a killer. What grounds do you have to interrogate him?"

Lily couldn't help but scowl. The Freeport police were supposed to be working with them, not against them.

"We have reason to believe he was involved in an incident on his boat that could've led to a woman's murder."

"A woman's murder!?"

Lily nodded. "We found damage to his boat with the same kind of aluminum used to repair a woman's boat that was found out at sea with a dead body on it." That was all she needed for now. It was enough to bring him in, anyway.

"Is that true, Professor? You had damage to your boat?"

"I don't know! Maybe I bumped something!"

The cop faced Lily again. "Well, we should talk to him. You Americans can stay out of it."

"Hey," Xander cut in, "we're with the FBI, asshole. We need to talk to him, and you can't stop us. You're under government orders to cooperate with the US forces—are you not?"

"My partner is right," Lily said. "You can't interfere with our investigation."

"We're not going to interfere," one of the police officers said. "But if you're going to interrogate this man, then we'll come along."

"Deal," Lily said. She couldn't care less.

She just wanted answers.

CHAPTER TWENTY THREE

This time in the interrogation room, Lily and Xander had an accomplice—Lily didn't like the way the police officer was standing by the door, arms crossed over his chest like he was their babysitter. He was listening to every moment of the interrogation, and it all rubbed Lily the wrong way.

It wouldn't be the first time that she'd seen corrupt police in her years as an FBI agent, and if Pinder had a brother on the force, then maybe these guys would be inclined to protect him.

Still, Lily had to remind herself to stay focused and do her job. If the police wanted to protect a killer, they were in for another story—the FBI would move hell and earth to get this guy behind bars.

First, Lily had to prove it was him.

"How did you get the mark on your boat, Mr. Pinder?" Lily asked, staring him down from across the table. "Was it a recent collision?"

He shook his head. "It certainly wasn't recently. I don't know how it got there."

"You don't remember hitting another boat? Or even accidentally bumping yours against a dock in the middle of the night?"

He looked at the floor and shook his head again.

"Because you were drunk," Lily said, but this time it had less of an accusation tone to it. "Is that why you have so much anxiety—because you think we're coming after you for boating while intoxicated?"

"I'm not drunk!" he protested, but Lily noticed that his eyes were bloodshot. Maybe it wasn't alcohol, maybe it was some other drug.

"I . . . I don't know what you're talking about."

"Yeah, you do," Xander said. "You've been so careful this whole time that you decided to take the chance and drive your boat over to Megan Frost's boat and hit her when she wasn't looking."

Pinder shook his head. "I promise I didn't do anything to anyone! I'd never hurt anyone! You have to believe me! I'm an astronomer; I have this love of the stars. This is my dream . . . of studying them up close. Who's going to take my boat away from me?"

"Who indeed?" Lily asked. She was trying to make a connection in her head, but she couldn't quite substantiate Pinder's guilt yet—at least not enough to prove it to a jury. Then again, just getting him arrested was enough right now. She had every intention of fleshing it out in court; this guy had some bizarre kind of map obsession, and if they could tie him to the murders, they were good to go.

"Listen," Xander said, "we don't want to take your boat away from you. We know boats are a business and losing a boat like this—even if it is just a hobby—you lose a lot. We can help cover the costs of getting it fixed."

"That's right," Lily echoed. "We don't want to take anything from you. Frankly, you're too unstable to be out on the ocean, anyway."

She could tell Pinder was on his last thread here. While he seemed genuinely concerned about the damage to his boat, she knew there was something else rattling around in that head of his. Something he didn't even want to admit to himself—and certainly not to them.

"I haven't done anything wrong," Pinder said. "You have no right to accuse me of killing."

"We have enough right," Xander said. "And believe me, we can get the evidence we need to put you away for life."

Pinder nervously shook his head. "You're telling me I might die in prison. This is insane!" He looked over at the police officer in the room and forced out a few short sobs. "This is all insane! I didn't kill anyone! I can't go to prison!"

The Freeport police officer said, "Hey, everything is going to be OK, Professor. Just answer their questions."

"You don't understand," Pinder said. "I use my teachings for good. There is so much to understand about how our ancestors used the sea and the stars. There's a connection, you see, a connection between the two—I would never hurt anyone. My life's goal is to teach this philosophy to anyone who will listen, and I love my students—I'd never hurt anyone, especially not any young women!"

The strange thoughts on the sea and the stars were what Lily was looking for. The killer was laying out a map of a constellation on the sea, using dead girls as markers. This guy's strange philosophy fit the bill.

"Where did the collision come from, Mr. Pinder?" Lily asked again.

"I told you, I don't—" He took a breath and sighed. "Damn it. Fine. I will tell you, but this could . . . it could ruin my credibility as a professor."

Lily exchanged a look with Xander. Where was he going with this?

"Look, I . . . I bumped into a student's boat while I was trying to dock at her place on the water. Her name is Sera Raye. She is a student in my class. Go look at her boat. You will see the mark from where I hit it. It was an accident."

Lily lifted an eyebrow. "Why were you going to a student's house?"

Pinder's face went red. "I . . ."

All at once, it clicked for Lily. Of course. "You were sleeping with her."

He hung his head low in shame.

"You're a dirty bastard, aren't you?" Xander said.

Lily tried to get a hold of herself. Was he trying to hurt a student? It was hard enough covering up affairs with teachers, but Pinder's position made it even worse. He could get fired for this behavior. Worse—he could get sued for harassment and lose everything he had.

If he didn't have an ax to grind with women . . .

Lily shook off the thought before she let it take control. Think about the case.

She went in for the kill: "Is that why you killed Megan Frost? Because she was going to ruin your career? Did she see you with Sera? What about Marie and Sophia?"

His head was still down, but one tear rolled out of his left eye and started gliding down his face, leaving a trail on his cheek. "I don't know any of these names . . . I didn't kill any women, I swear it."

"You're a liar," Lily said. "There's only one direction for this Star Cult nonsense—the sea. You use the sea as a map, and you use these women as victims."

"No! No! I'm an astronomer, I swear to you. I'm an instructor at Freeport Academy of the Sciences and I love what I do."

Lily studied him—with his pained expression and tears in his eyes, he seemed genuine. And he was vulnerable, putting himself out there like that.

Lily's gut twisted. In a weird way, she was starting to doubt Pinder's guilt. They would have to confirm with Sera—that was the first step.

But her intuition wasn't quite sure, either.

"This is all bullshit," Xander said to Pinder. "Maybe your little student would cover your ass. You smell dirty, Pinder. We know you did this, and we'll find the proof we need."

What should I do? Lily asked herself. *He seems so genuinely scared and confused, but if he's lying to us, I can't let him get away with it.*

"I didn't hurt anyone," Pinder said. His voice started wavering, and his eyes moved to the floor. "Please, let me go."

"We'll let you go, all right," Xander said. "Straight into a prison cell."

Lily could tell he had already made up his mind, but she had to trust her own gut too. They had to check this Sera person's boat. They had to talk to her.

Lily stood up, gaining a confused look from Xander. He clearly wasn't done, but Lily was. "You'll remain in custody until we can verify your story, Mr. Pinder," Lily said. Xander shot her a look like he was pissed that she'd made this call when he still wanted to ask more. Lily ignored him and turned to the door, heading out of the interrogation room, and gaining a look from the officer standing guard. She landed in the hallway, and Xander sped out after her.

"What the hell, Dawn?" he asked once they were alone. "I wasn't done in there!"

"Jackson, we need to confirm his story," Lily said. "If he did hit Sera's boat, we'll see that. He might not be our guy, and if he isn't, then we can't waste any more time."

"But he's guilty," Xander said. "He's covering up something, and I don't trust killers to tell the truth."

What about the truth? Lily's gut asked. Her anger and frustration were getting away from her. This case was spinning in circles. They'd gotten more information when she was just using logic and observation. Now that she was concerned with emotions, she lost her center. What if her gut was too weak?

No. She had to trust herself. And she needed her partner to have faith in her too.

"That boat could give us some answers," Lily said. "If Pinder isn't our guy, we should clear him ASAP and focus on the next lead before we lose another girl. Don't you think?"

“Yes, I just—this guy seems like he’s the one,” Xander sighed, obviously annoyed by the detour. “But you’re right. Let’s go check out his story, then we nail him.”

CHAPTER TWENTY FOUR

He crept alongside the cruise ship on the dock, which was moored down at the bay, just as the sun was descending toward the horizon. Up close, the vessel was even more magnificent than he had seen from afar, and he couldn't wait to get on board and take his pick of the lot.

One of the girls here would be coming with him, joining him on his vessel, and becoming one of his forever stars. She would be so lucky to be chosen by him in this cosmic task.

But first, he had to sneak on the ship.

He slowed down and gave a raspy sigh in frustration, mixed in with the crowd of people on the dock. He was cautious by nature and didn't want to be caught sneaking around on the boat. That would end badly for a man like him, especially since he wasn't even supposed to be here.

There's no way I'll be able to get on board without security noticing me, he thought.

A gentle ocean breeze floated by, taking with it his fears, as he watched the sun sink deeply into the glittering sea below him.

Maybe I can swim up to the deck instead. They'll never be looking in the water, he thought, growing excited at the prospect of finally meeting his brand-new star after all these hours of watching her distant twinkling in the night sky. This girl's destiny had been waiting for her inside that glowing star, waiting for his ship to come by and whisk her away, but she didn't know it.

He went to the end of the dock and glanced over his shoulder. There were many people here, many who had hopped off the cruise ship. This was his chance. While most of the people were away, he could choose from the remaining pool. His boat was waiting just up the shore, and the sun was setting. It would be dark soon. He could use that to shield himself as he dragged her through the water. He would have to keep her quiet, but he had a plan.

When no one was looking, he slipped into the cool water below, weighed down by his clothes, but he didn't care. This plan was so much bigger than him—it would be worth it in the end.

The water was eerily cold, chilling his bones as he submerged. It was easier to float than he had imagined, but still hard enough to swim against. He pulled himself forward by the surface of the water and kicked his feet back as he went.

It had been a while since he swam, but he was determined not to turn back until he had his prize. One more strong kick gave him the momentum to whip out into the beyond; it wasn't too far. A final big stroke brought him through the cool water and up onto the ship's deck in one final lap. He treaded water quietly, waiting for his heart to slow its pace before climbing up onto the side of the ship's ladder with ease.

He pulled himself over and out of the water, drenched from head to toe. But this wouldn't be a problem for much longer. The deck of the cruise ship was empty—even the staff weren't on this part. He could hear merriment from down the hall, a celebration of sorts going on inside.

He saw a pair of shoes and a handbag lying on a lounge chair, and then a pile of clothes on the floor. He recognized the shawl, as well, that was thrown over the side. This could be his girl, but where was she? This might not be as simple as he'd planned. He had hoped to simply grab a girl, pull her overboard, and swim away, but it might take more planning than that.

Just then, a voice. He pressed his back to the wall of the ship and took a breath. Someone was coming.

He peered around the corner onto the main deck. And there he saw it: a male staffer, wearing a white uniform. He could knock him out and steal his clothes.

Then he would really blend in. The cruise-goers would never know he was not an employee. The employee was heading right for his hiding place—either he saw him or heard his approach.

He'd have to strike fast.

The employee rounded the corner, and that was when he struck.

He bashed him over the back of the head with his fist, so hard that the young man dropped. Assured that no one else was there, he slipped out of his clothes, then tossed them over the railing of the ship. No reason to leave wet clothes lying around. He slipped the white uniform on—it didn't fit him well, but it would do for now. He shoved the employee into a supply closet, just as he heard voices coming from another part of the cruise ship.

Female voices.

Girls, having fun on their cruise.

With the benefit of disguise, he came out of hiding and walked across the beautiful deck of the cruise ship where some of the people staying on the ship began to return from their trip into Freeport. He noticed a girl, walking alone, her eyes glued to her cellphone. She wasn't one of the ones he'd picked while observing the boat, but if he could get her alone, away from the group, then she would do just perfectly.

A smile curled at his lips. It was getting dark now.

He kept to the shadows, observing the crowd as they descended from the ship with drinks in their hands. They were as taken with the sunset as anyone else. The girl he had chosen was off her phone, leaning her elbows over the railing, watching the scene.

All he had to do was bide his time.

Then, he would strike.

CHAPTER TWENTY FIVE

Lily and Xander stood at the edge of the beach as darkness swept over the sky, and Lily's stomach was completely in knots. Behind them, Sera Raye's boat was docked at the home she lived at with her parents. They'd taken their own boat here, and it was docked on the water, waiting for them to get back in, because there was nothing left for them to do here.

Sera's boat had a dent in it, just like the professor had claimed it would. That could only mean that his story was, at the very least, probable. Forensics was currently examining the material found on the professor's boat to confirm if the chipped paint on it could have come from Megan's boat, but it was looking more and more unlikely.

Even Xander had started to accept that truth.

"Damn it," Xander said, staring out at the ocean. It was getting late, and Lily knew the clock was ticking. "Now what the hell do we do?"

Lily leaned toward their boat. "We need to go back to the drawing board. We were close with the professor—but it's not him, so we have to re-examine what we know."

They went back to the boat and got settled in, but Lily didn't start the engine. She didn't want to go anywhere until she had a solid destination.

She took out her phone, opening up the killer's pattern on the water, re-examining it. Her phone lit the darkening night as she zoomed in. Xander stood up on the boat and leaned over her shoulder, watching.

"If we could figure out the constellation, we could pinpoint where he's going to strike next," Lily said.

"Here." Xander took his phone out and loaded a map of constellations.

She cross-referenced them again, but none of them started with the pattern he had laid out.

"None of these look right—I don't know what he's looking for," she said, frustrated. The killer seemed so close and yet so far. Now that they had lost the professor, logic gave way to desperation.

They needed to pull back a bit. What could they tell about this killer's pathology? What was it like to be in his mind?

"What do we know so far," Lily mused, thinking out loud. She leaned in the captain's chair of the speedboat and held her thumb to her chin. "The three victims are all Americans. All brown-haired and white. At least two of them had an affinity for sailing. We can assume our killer does too. And now we know the killer is interested in stars and constellations."

Xander grunted in frustration. "I was so damn sure that professor was our guy."

"It did seem to be on the right track," Lily said. "The way he was talking about using the stars as a map to guide one's self through the sea . . . it can't be a coincidence."

A cool wind blew over the sea. Lily looked at the pattern again. She flipped the image around as if a different perspective might help.

"Xander," she said. "Pull up the constellation chart again."

He did as he was told.

With this new perspective, Lily glanced through the constellations again.

Hold on . . .

She squinted. A thought suddenly rushed her. She'd been looking for the beginnings of a constellation as though the killer would start from the top.

But if she looked at the pattern from a horizontal viewpoint, she could see that the dots lined up with three different points of the Little Dipper. Just not in order.

Lily's head spun. Was she seeing this right?

"Xander," Lily said. "Look at this." She pointed to the layout of the Little Dipper. Three different points hovered around one of the stars. Two stars were one point, then a gap to the third. "You know the Little Dipper?"

"The pattern of the stars in it," he said, looking at her for a moment before connecting them. "Son of a . . ."

The killer wasn't looking just for constellations—he was looking for something specific in that constellation between three stars. A pattern unique not just to each victim, but specific to a star.

He was building the Little Dipper, but he was not doing it in order.

"The little dipper has six stars in it," Lily said. "That means—"

"Three different spots this bastard could be taking a girl tonight," Xander said.

"Exactly. At the rate he's been accelerating, another girl will die tonight," Lily said. Her heart pounded. "We need to get to all three of these locations."

"We can't be everywhere at the same time," Xander said. "We're gonna need to split up, Dawn."

Lily's heart had never been so tight. "Get the coast guard on the phone."

*

The lights of Lily's boat cut through the night as she sliced through the darkness of the sea, manning a boat alone for the first time in years.

Xander was with the coast guard, heading to the other two locations. Lily was on her own in this.

The closer she came to the first spot, the more silent and still it became. She was heading out to sea, into the field of stars. It was dark behind her. The lights on her boat were the only guiding factor. If she shut them off, she would be swallowed by blackness and floating in space.

Some part of her kept expecting a hail of bullets to mask out of nowhere, and that the killer would suddenly jump out of the shadows and into her boat, stringing her up like the others.

But instead, there was nothing but silence . . . haunting silence. The lights guided her, lighting up dark water and stars above. The sound of the speedboat's motor was too loud, and the lights were too bright. As Lily drew closer to the location, which she kept open on the GPS on her phone, she knew she had to turn it all off soon so as not to give away her location.

Her heart pounded in her ears. They didn't know if he'd be going there, or was already there, or how long they might have to wait. Either way, Lily knew she was facing a long night out at sea, and the thought sent a chill through her.

As she made her way through the night, she couldn't stop the onslaught of memories. Out here, under the clear blanket of stars, she couldn't help but remember the night Kara had gone missing.

Back in Aruba, life had been so different for Lily. She had never imagined she would grow up to be an FBI agent. In fact, in her teen years, Lily had been more of a free-spirited party animal than anything else.

She liked drinking with friends and spending late nights out. She had one boyfriend after another—none of them were serious. She had fun and wanted to explore the world. Her parents had disapproved of her behavior, but Lily didn't care; she was young and carefree, but meanwhile, Kara was more bookish and school smart. She cared about her grades and aced every test. Lily's parents were always worried that as they got older, Lily's partying would rub off on Kara in the wrong way.

Then, one night, when Lily was seventeen and Kara was sixteen, Kara decided she finally wanted to go out and party with Lily and her friends.

Lily was reluctant to get her little sister involved with the party world, but the two made a deal: Lily and her friends would take Kara on a cruise through Aruba that night, and if she could handle it, she could come out and party again later.

The first part of the night had been much like any other night—drinking out by the beach, having a great time.

Kara hung out with the other girls and followed them around, laughing at all the boys who sprayed her with coconut sunscreen. Lily was careful not to give her too much to drink, just in case.

But at a certain point in the night, Lily had gotten too drunk. She remembered partying with this guy she liked and taking shots straight from the bottle as they spread out on towels under the magnificent night sky. Aruba was so gorgeous. Lily had been intoxicated by the alcohol, by the guy, and by how beautiful the night was. She remembered lying on his chest, tuning out the world . . .

Then she woke up, and suddenly the sun was out, and the party had completely left the beach. Lily and her date had passed out drunk on the beach, and no one came to wake them up.

Suddenly completely sober, Lily had stood up and brushed sand off her.

Where the hell was Kara?

Oh, shit! The awareness hit her like a tsunami. Lily ran home as fast as she could. Even now, as an FBI agent, she had never felt such panic. Her parents had trusted her to take Kara out that night. Lily just prayed that when she got home, Kara would be there waiting.

Lily dove into the house. Her parents were at work, so no one was home.

Not even Kara.

Lily's heart had wanted to leap from her chest. She was panicking. She called her friends from the party the night before, and everyone said the last place they saw Kara was on the beach.

Kara was gone.

And Lily spent the entire day searching their town, searching the beach, searching everywhere.

Kara was never found.

Now, as the memories of missing Kara rushed Lily again, she prayed that the night's chaos would not end just as tragically for another girl tonight.

The cold wind whipped at Lily's face, sending goosebumps prancing down her arms. Her parents never forgave her for losing track of Kara that night, and in truth, Lily never forgave herself. She cleaned up her act after that and had her eyes on law enforcement before she decided she'd move to the USA and join the FBI. Lily couldn't find her sister, but she wanted to dedicate her life to saving other people, so no one else ever had to disappear again.

The pain and guilt of Kara's disappearance would stay with Lily forever. No matter what, she was not going to let that happen again tonight.

If it was the last thing she did, she would stop this man, or at least give their families some peace as they grieved their losses.

The location on her GPS was coming up.

Almost there.

CHAPTER TWENTY SIX

After a long, lonely cruise where Lily constantly checked the GPS and watched the stars, she found the spot where he might be.

She cut the engine and coasted into the dark water. Lily waited on the speedboat for a few minutes, trying to gather her nerves. She checked the time on her phone. If Xander had gotten his location correct, and they were all converging on these spots at once, they had a huge chance at cornering him.

If they were too late, though, another girl would be killed tonight.

Lily couldn't let that happen.

This was it.

Lily guided the boat slowly through the sea. The darkness was dense here, with the clouds shielding the moon and stars, and she couldn't see a thing. A flashlight would only reveal Lily's location for the killer to target.

She hadn't considered that until now. Her heart had been hammering from the moment she turned off her boat's lights and got closer to this location. Now, the full weight of everything was sinking in, and Lily felt like this dark sea was rising up to swallow her.

But she forced herself on.

Lily was going on her gut instinct; she felt like if this was where the killer would strike next, he wouldn't wait too long. These parts were quiet, and he would think he could slip through undetected.

But this time, someone would be waiting. Whether he came here, or to one of the other two locations, Lily didn't know. Either way, he would be caught.

He had to be.

Lily took a breath as she drifted further along the sea . . . and that was when she saw it.

A vessel, up ahead.

A white boat.

Her heart stalled. No, that was no coast guard boat.

Lily sucked in a breath. She had to be sure it wasn't an ordinary civilian. She couldn't just attack.

She pulled out a pair of binoculars and peered through them. As if on cue, a cloud parted from the moon, giving enough pearly light to illuminate the boat.

Lily's heart dropped into her stomach.

On the boat, there was a man steering.

And next to him, lying on the bench of the boat, was an unconscious young woman. Lily wanted to drop her binoculars as the cold realization hit her like a bullet. Her instincts had been right. This was the right place at the right time, but maybe she was too late. Maybe the girl was already dead.

Lily picked up her radio and said, "This is Agent Dawn. I have eyes on him at my location. Requesting immediate backup."

Now came the hard part—attacking this man when he wasn't expecting it and also not alerting him to her presence in the water. She couldn't take a shot directly, because she had no idea if he could turn around and kill the girl—and she couldn't risk shooting her in the process. She couldn't just fall into his trap this easily.

No, she had to come up with another plan.

And fast.

Lily watched the boat. She saw the killer fiddling with some rope on the boat—maybe that was what he'd use to tie her up.

"No," Lily muttered under her breath.

She knew the drill: get closer, get the girl on her boat, and get out of there fast.

Cautiously, Lily pulled her boat closer to the boat where the killer was.

That was when the clouds blew in again, concealing the moonlight and plunging the sea back into darkness.

Shit.

The only way she could know for sure whether or not that girl was dead was to go on board, but if she didn't do it now, this guy might spot her. Lily took out the binoculars again, and that was when she saw it: the girl was waking up.

The man glanced at the girl next to him.

And struck her unconscious again with a good blow to her head.

Anger tore through Lily. No! To hell with this—she couldn't wait any longer. She had to save this girl, and so she revved up her engine and flicked on her lights, beaming in on the man like a giant spotlight.

He looked back in horror. Lily could finally get a good look at him—he was short, squat, and overweight, with a balding head. He must have been in his fifties, and he was white—potentially American.

Lily's teeth grit. She sped right after him, but he didn't waste any time, either. He dove behind his wheel and kicked on his engine.

And just like that, Lily's boat was chasing his through the dark, open seas.

Lily was ready to jump in, but she had to get closer. The air flew through her hair as she sped after him, the sound of their motors cutting into the night.

The killer was heading back southeast, away from the town. He probably thought he could get away from her—but Lily wasn't about to let that happen. She plunged after the killer, letting out a scream when a wave crashed against her side, sending water spraying into the air. But Lily held steady. The killer kicked on his speed, starting to get a lead.

Lily clenched her teeth. She couldn't let him get away like this. It would be too dangerous to come after this man again. She forced herself on, trying to speed in pursuit of him. The killer was hauling butt now, jamming his engine into drive and running through the water as fast as he could push it.

Bastard, she thought. *You bastard—I won't let you kill her!*

Lily sped even faster—but the killer started to speed away, speeding out of range.

The killer glanced over his shoulder, and his face was that of shock. Lily wouldn't give up. She saw him turning through the open waters, and she made a beeline straight for him.

Lily felt herself getting closer. He wasn't going to get away.

Moments like these were her salvation. The reason she became an FBI agent. Lily would never forgive herself for what happened to Kara, but she would fight tooth and nail to save others, and that was all she could do.

Whoever this guy was, he would pay for his crimes.

Lily could see his boat was losing steam while hers pushed on, full speed ahead, cutting through the water like a knife. She was scant feet away from him. A hundred feet away . . . fifty . . . her boat was about to crash into his if she didn't make a move. Maybe he was taunting her to do it, because he kept on course, occasionally looking back. Lily had no choice but to swerve, and when she did, he swerved in the other direction.

She revved her engine and headed straight after him.

"FBI! Freeze!"

He was a slow learner, but he began to pick up the pace.

Lily kept her eyes on him. "FBI! I'm warning you—I have a gun!"

He still didn't look like he believed her. He glanced over his shoulder at Lily, his boat trailing behind him. He turned back to her, and Lily whipped forward in pursuit. Then suddenly, the killer killed his engine and let his boat slow. Lily kept on him, thinking maybe he'd made a mistake.

And that was when Lily realized her mistake. He'd played her so perfectly, and she'd fallen for it hook, line, and sinker. His boat stopped dead in the water, and Lily's only a second behind him. And just like that, the killer whirled around on her.

Lily didn't have time to pull the trigger before three gunshots rang out, one right after the other, each one crashing into Lily's vessel like a bullet. Her ears screamed at the sudden noise, and the glass inside the cabin shattered—but somehow, despite all this, Lily's focus remained on what mattered.

She punched a hole through the last barrier between her and this man—there was just enough time to catch sight of his face as she aimed her gun straight for him. She shot his arm, and he dropped the gun, sending it flying into the water. Lily's boat was compromised—it slowly sank into the water, but she pushed forward, using the last of its momentum to get closer to his boat. The man grabbed his bleeding arm, reeling from the pain, giving her time to get the advantage on him.

Her vessel pulled up beside his.

Lily didn't give him a chance to grab for another weapon. It was time to get this guy.

She jumped off her own boat and landed right on his.

CHAPTER TWENTY SEVEN

The man yelled out in shock, just as Lily dropped right next to him. Up close, she got a good view of his face: ugly and twisted with rage, and his eyes were full of a strange, deranged emotion.

This man was dangerous. Lily felt it in every fiber of her being.

The wind whirred around them. Lily held her gun on him firmly, and he stared her down like he was completely unafraid.

"Don't move," Lily said firmly. "FBI. You're under arrest."

The boat rocked beneath them. The man's arm was bleeding, but he showed no emotion.

Lily couldn't resist the gnaw of curiosity.

"Who are you?"

The man didn't say a word, but he narrowed his eyes. Lily could almost feel his anger as he looked at her.

Then there was a sudden shift in the air. She could feel it. Something was going to happen, something terrible, she could feel it . . . and she knew—

She didn't want to know what he would say, but she had to know.

"Who are you?" Lily's teeth clenched together. "Why have you been killing women?" The words were fired directly at the man. Blood dripped from his arm onto the boat, but still he refused to say a word. His face remained stoic as stone.

The man said absolutely nothing, watching Lily steadily. It was unnerving, and it made the hair on the back of her neck stand up.

"Damn it!" she cried. "Who are you?" But once again, it was like trying to communicate with a brick wall. The man twisted his face into a grin, and this was a sight that struck fear into Lily's heart. His eyes bulged, and the corners of his mouth opened.

In one quick movement, the man reached for something. Lily didn't think—she just shot. She pegged him in the shoulder, but it didn't stop him.

He charged her, a knife in his hand.

Lily was quick to aim, but she wasn't quick enough. The killer plunged his blade into her arm, and Lily dropped her weapon. Fiery hot pain shot up her arm, causing her to wince. The boat rocked, sending her gun sliding to the other side, past the unconscious girl.

The sharp pain was nothing compared to the shock—this man had just stabbed her.

Lily stumbled backwards. The killer slashed his knife through the air, getting ready for the next strike that would settle this. Lily didn't waste any time—she pulled herself back onto her boat, going for another weapon.

But the killer continued after her.

"You want to know who I am!?" he began. "I'm a pioneer. I'm an astronomer. More than that—I'm a father!" He tackled Lily, and she dodged around him, avoiding his blade.

But the killer grabbed her by the hand, clutching her arm in a death grip that Lily could not escape. He held her up at blade point.

"I'm getting my daughter back!" he screamed, his voice laced with pain. "She's not yours! She's mine!"

Lily sent her knee up and got him in the gut, sending him backwards. They both steadied themselves on the boat, but the man stood between Lily and her gun. *Damn it.*

"What the hell are you talking about?" Lily said.

"My daughter," he said. "I'm just guiding her home. She can read the stars in the sea. I'll see her again. I'll see Janie."

His eyes became moist with emotion. Real or not, he was as crazy as a loon.

The man began to swing his knife again. Lily tried to get to her feet, but her arm wasn't working properly. It was barely functional. She lurched upwards, and the killer lunged right after her.

He dipped Lily's head down and brought his pocketknife down toward her neck. Lily reacted by shoving him off her.

At that moment, lights appeared in the distance. Boats coming their way.

The coast guard—and Xander.

Lily allowed herself a moment of relief, but she couldn't hold onto it. This wasn't over. The deranged man ran at her with the knife again, and this time, Lily dodged around him. She needed to get that gun.

"I will get my daughter back," the man uttered. "And if you get in my way—I'll make you one of my stars too."

From the corner of her eye, she saw the coast guard boats. Xander was in one of them. She couldn't get their attention now—the killer would kill her before they'd had a chance to act.

Lily looked him in the eyes as he held up the knife. The wind whipped her hair in all directions. The gun was behind him, and if she could just get him to move, she could dive at it and subdue him. But he wasn't budging.

Maybe the best way to stop this was to get in his head. He'd said he had a daughter.

"Janie," Lily said, and his nostrils flared. "Who is she?"

"My daughter," he said. "She was lost, lost at sea, but she's going to come home once she reads my message."

Lily swallowed hard. "You mean the constellation you're building? You think she will read it?"

His nostrils flared. "So, that is how you found me . . ." He laughed once, then looked up at the sky. "Yes, Janie will see. She will see, and she will find her way home."

"But Janie's dead, isn't she?" Lily countered.

His eyes snapped to hers, full of rage. "Do not say that. She isn't dead. She's just lost."

The man laughed again. "Once she sees that star map, once I show her . . ."

His voice became tired, and Lily knew she was getting closer. His eyes started revealing more sadness than anger, and Lily pressed on. She had to keep him talking.

"What did you promise Janie when she got older?" Lily made herself stand as tall as possible, looking him straight in the eyes.

"She loved the sea," he said. "We went sailing together." His eyes became glassy with emotion, but he blinked them away quickly, steeling his emotions back into the present. Until they would be useful again.

"But if Janie's dead, then why are you still doing this?" Lily asked. "You know she won't read it. You know she's gone."

There was a long silence. The man kept his face passive, but Lily could see the turmoil on his face, anger and misery mingling together into a sea of emotions.

And then, finally, he spoke. His voice was quiet, but when he spoke, all other sound was silenced. His words rang true and clear, a solid explosion that ripped through the wind and shook the very atmosphere. "She is not gone," he said. "I can feel her. She's out there, lost, and she needs her father to guide her home. She needs stars . . . beautiful girls like her."

Lily's heart clenched. This was why he had been choosing the young American tourists, all with brown hair.

The coast guard ships were getting closer. If Lily could keep him talking just a little longer, she could end this without bloodshed.

"Janie's gone," she said. "She's not coming home. By killing these girls, you're killing other people's daughters. Is that what Janie would want?"

The man's lips smiled again. "These girls are stars for my beautiful Janie."

"But she's already gone," Lily said, willing her voice not to break. "That's why you're doing this—you have to accept it."

His face became tortured, and she felt all his rational thoughts slip away into the fiery pits of emotional outrage. His eyes reddened, and the blade he held was dripping with the blood of the girls who were lost like his daughter.

The man's mouth opened, and he screamed.

Then he charged, knife held high. Lily dodged at the last possible moment, and plunged on him, tackling him back onto the boat as they both hit. The weapon slipped from his hand and clattered on the boat's side ramp, and both of them toppled over, landing on the floor of the boat. He tried to grab her, but Lily shoved him away, and then they were both unarmed and facing each other on the boat.

"She will come home!" he shouted, and Lily took a step closer to the gun left lying just beyond her reach. "Mark my words! I built that constellation for her. I took her star out of the sky, and I put it on earth! She'll find her way here."

He glared at her. Lily went cold—the look in his eyes had changed drastically. A madness unlike any she had seen before. A crazed mania that would threaten everyone on this boat.

As she reached for her gun, he charged her again, grabbing the knife, and this time, Lily had to shoot. She fired. The gunshot resounded through the air. It went right through his shoulder. Lily wasn't going for the kill; she just wanted to subdue and arrest him.

And it worked.

He grabbed at his shoulder and fell to the floor, eyes full of shock. Lily stepped forward to cuff him, but then he stiffened. He turned his head to stare at her—not with anger or malice, but with an emotion that sent shivers down her spine: eyes empty of focus.

"Lily!" a voice shouted, and Lily looked up to see Xander's boat ripping up to them. Behind him, a coast guard ship was close, its lights cutting through the night.

But the killer was slumped on the floor, blood pouring from his shoulder and staring at her blankly as if he didn't even see her. He was having some sort of stare-off with Lily, so she couldn't shoot him again. She couldn't risk hurting him further. So, she slapped cuffs on him and then stood up straight.

It might just be the adrenaline playing tricks on her mind but looking at him—so broken and helpless—and waiting for Xander to hit them with the boat, she realized that she felt sorry for this man.

She had almost killed a man who wanted nothing more than to see his daughter again. Still, nothing would erase his crimes.

Snapping out of it, Lily ran over to the unconscious girl and checked her pulse. She was alive and breathing, and Lily let out a breath of relief.

"Lily!" Xander shouted behind her, coming neatly up to their boat. Lily turned around to see him boarding, along with another coast guard officer, who grabbed the killer. Xander hurried up to Lily, concern on his face, lit by the moonlight between the clouds. He looked down at her holding the girl and let out a breath.

Lily couldn't help but almost smile.

"We did it, Jackson," she said.

He let out a massive laugh. "You're damn right we did."

CHAPTER TWENTY EIGHT

The sun shone in Lily's eyes as she, along with Xander, stepped into the Freeport police station the next morning. It had been a hell of a night. Getting the killer into custody and explaining everything that had happened to both the coast guard and the Freeport police had taken a lot out of Lily, and even Xander was tired. In the end, though, they'd passed responsibility of the killer off to the others, and Xander and Lily had gone back to their place exhausted and slept for only a couple of hours.

Now, they were here for answers.

Entering the quiet building, they moved through the hall to meet with the head of police and Officer Chandler, who was representing the coast guard. The two men waited in a small room at the end of the hall, which Lily knocked on before both she and Xander entered.

Officer Chandler stood up from his spot at the chair and offered each Lily and Xander a hand.

"Agent Dawn, Agent Jackson," he said. "This is Commissioner Jordan."

Commissioner Jordan stood up and offered them a hand, too, which they both shook. He was short man, a native islander with dark skin and eyes that had seen many crimes. Lily had seen that look before.

"Thank you for what you've done," said the commissioner. "I can see that working with the FBI was the right move here."

"It was a pleasure," Xander said. "Sir." He then smiled. "Not always the easiest job, but it's not bad to have backup to rely on sometimes."

Commissioner Jordan tilted his head. "You face unique challenges as an FBI agent?"

Xander laughed. "That I do, sir. The FBI and the FPD are historical enemies, it always makes for some crazy moments when we have to work together. Good for the publicity and all, but I sleep easier knowing I have backup."

Jordan smiled, appreciating Xander's humor. "Well, let me assure you both that as long as you remain in Freeport, you have my full trust."

"Thank you, sir," Lily said. As much as she appreciated the light mood, there were many questions that were burning in her. "What do we know about him?"

"His name's Alexander Royce," said Jordan. "He's an American from Florida. His daughter, Janice, recently passed away—drowned while she was swimming on the beaches of Florida."

Janice was Janie, the daughter he'd brought up. Lily knew she shouldn't feel bad for the sorry bastard after what he'd done, but still. This was a complicated situation, and she could see that Alexander had experienced something that made him lose touch with reality.

"So, what brought him here?" Lily asked.

"We're not really sure," Officer Chandler said. "Maybe he thought he could get away with it here off US soil."

"Well, he was wrong," Xander said.

Lily looked at him. Even though this had been a tough case for him, the fact that he hadn't taken it harder really wasn't something she expected of him. She found herself thankful for that.

"He's going to receive the maximum sentence," Chandler said, catching Lily off-guard with her emotion. "I'm glad. This one hit close to home for me. I have a daughter too."

Xander and Lily nodded, somberly. If a case could bring the people who worked so hard to keep the peace together, Lily really couldn't condemn them for doing that.

"I'm just glad this is all over," Lily said.

"Likewise," said the commissioner. "Are you two going back to America?"

"Yes," Lily said. As soon as the case had been solved, the FBI made arrangements for Lily to get on a private jet. She was leaving this afternoon.

"I'm gonna stick around for a couple days," Xander said, and Lily shot him a look. She had no idea he planned on staying in Freeport, but then again, they hadn't spoken much since taking down Royce. They were too tired, and there had been too much chaos for idle chitchat.

"Well, thanks, you two," Chandler said. "You were a great asset here."

Lily nodded, thanking them again. With that, she and Xander left the office. They made their way outside into the warm, humid day and back to the rental car. Xander got behind the wheel, and Lily sat in the passenger seat. She paused for a moment before she faced him.

"What are you staying for?"

A smile crossed his lips. "Someone I used to know always wanted to vacation here. Guess I wanted to do a little sight-seeing. For her."

Her? Lily wondered, but she didn't ask. It was Xander's business, and although they'd grown to accept each other more, they weren't at the level of friendship yet.

The car started, and Xander made his way back to their place so Lily could pack her bags and grab her flight.

As he drove, Xander mused, "I guess this is it, huh?"

Lily looked at him. The Bahamas sun reflected off his aviators as he drove.

"What's it?" Lily asked.

"Us. You and me. Partners." Xander glanced at her. "I gotta say, this was one of the shortest cases I've worked. You nailed this thing, Dawn."

Lily couldn't help but smile. "And you thought I was too young to be a good agent."

He shrugged. "You proved me wrong."

Lily frowned. "You're gonna miss me, aren't you?"

Xander let out as hearty laugh. "Hey, you're the one leaving. I'll be just fine without you."

A smile crossed her lips. "Dream on."

"Seriously, though, you're one hell of a shot and you've got a cool head. You're gonna go far in the FBI."

Lily laughed again, resting her forehead against the cool glass of the car window. She felt good knowing that she'd received so much positive reinforcement, especially coming from someone like Xander, but she couldn't help but feel bad that they might be on different paths.

Lily could tell already in Lily's training that she was destined to rise high in the FBI, no matter what mission they sent her on. But she wanted something more than that. She wasn't sure exactly what it was yet, but she was still looking.

"What about you?" Lily asked, looking at him again. "Where do you see yourself going?"

"I'm staying with the FBI," Xander answered. "It's really the only thing that I think I need in life. What else am I supposed to do? So many people try to rise in politics and end up becoming corrupt themselves. Or something else boring like that. Even if I don't land special agent soon, the FBI's my calling. I've done my time with the SEALs and all that, but this is where I feel most at home. So, once I'm done my little vacation, it's back to Florida for me."

Lily nodded. "Sounds like a good plan, Jackson."

She turned back around and watched the scenery rush past the window. She thought of her upcoming flight and going home to Quantico. But in reality, there was no home for her there. Sure, she had her apartment, but here, on these islands—this felt like home. She missed Aruba. She missed her parents . . . she missed Kara.

It had brought back a lot of dark memories, but Lily was glad she'd been able to come to this part of the world again. Leaving was bittersweet.

She glanced one last time at Xander, who wore a pleasant smile as they both reflected on their time together. Maybe he did count Lily as a friend after all.

CHAPTER TWENTY NINE

Lily stood on the runway, the afternoon sun shining bright. In front of her was her private jet, the stairs down, waiting for her to board. Lily had her luggage and all her stuff with her. Xander had just dropped her off, and now she stood alone under the Caribbean sun.

That feeling of sunlight on her face was something that felt so much like home to her.

With all the memories stirred up in her on this case, Lily had been thinking about something crazy for a little while now.

She wanted to call her parents.

It was a risky move, she knew that. They hadn't spoken to her in a year, since Kara was declared "legally dead," despite there being no body ever found. Before that, her parents had never forgiven her for taking Kara out that night—and losing her.

It was all Lily's fault. Even as she dedicated herself to the FBI, to doing good for the world, it would never be enough in her parents' eyes . . . or her own.

Lily hesitated, then took out her phone. With a deep breath, she dialed her father's number. She didn't even know for sure if this was his number anymore, but she waited for it to ring anyway.

On the other line, she could hear the phone ring three times before there was an answer.

"Hello?" asked a male voice that caused Lily's heart to skip a beat. It was her father. It was easy to forget, after a year without having contact, how much his voice had meant so much to her.

Lily paused again and had to try three times to get any words out of her mouth at all. Finally, she managed a soft, "H . . . hi Dad."

The line went silent. Then again, "Hello? Lily? Are you there?"

Heat rushed over Lily, making her face suddenly flush with blush. How would it be if she told him who she really was? There he was, still expecting an old memory to pick up the phone instead of the woman in the present. Wouldn't that hurt the man even more?

Her lips trembled as she looked around—for what, she wasn't sure.

"Dad, I'm here," Lily said.

There was silence on the other end of the phone. Lily could hear her father breathing, his deep exhalations on the line, and even though it was just a small detail, hearing someone's breathing like that felt like coming home again after such a long time apart.

She took a deep breath herself, mustering up all her courage, hoping her dad would talk to her again and be her father again after all this time.

"It's . . . surprising to hear from you," her father said. "Where are you? What's going on?"

"I'm in the Bahamas . . . for work."

"Ah," her father said. "You're so close to home."

Lily's heart bottomed out. Home. Her father still thought of Aruba as her home. She did too. In her heart, she always would.

"I have to return to Virginia," Lily said. "I was here on a case."

"Ah . . ." Her dad trailed off. "Did the case go well?"

"It did. We caught the killer and saved a woman."

"That is great, Lily."

"Thank you." She paused, her voice thick with emotion. "I was wondering if we could maybe arrange for me to come visit you and Mom soon. In Aruba."

The line was silent. Lily's heart started to ache as her father went on not answering the question, and she felt the silence start to go on too long.

"Are you still there?" she asked.

"Yes," her father said finally. "I was thinking about what you said."

"And?" Lily asked, trying to stay calm.

"I can talk to your mother," he said, then he started coughing profusely through the phone. Lily flinched. Her whole life, her father had been healthy and active—she'd rarely heard him cough, let alone with such intensity. "Dad, are you okay?"

He sighed as his coughing fit calmed. "Lily . . . I'm not doing well. My health has been declining recently, and we aren't sure why."

Panic struck her. "Is it . . . cancer?" Lily asked, her voice trembling.

"Possibly," he said. "There's something on my lungs. I'm being seen by a doctor, but I'm starting to get weaker every day, and I don't have time to wait to see what they find in the end."

Lily's mind was reeling as she tried to process this new information. She couldn't imagine a life without her parents, but so much time had passed, and they didn't even know who she was any more due to Lily not really existing in the eyes of their world she had pulled Kara into. Now cancer might take him before she'd even had a chance to talk to him and her mother again.

"Lily?"

"I'm here, Dad," she said, snapping out of it. "I want to come visit you." This time, she had to be firm.

"I would like that," her dad said. "Let me talk to your mother."

Hope could be dangerous, but Lily allowed herself to feel it. To feel like maybe her mom would let her come home, and she'd see her dad before things got worse.

Acknowledging and talking to her father again gave her hope in another way too. Not only would she be able to see him again, but it'd give Lily the push she needed to keep going in life. Because at this moment she realized, even if Kara hadn't come back, Lily couldn't give up.

Because finally, fearlessly, she had found something to live for again.

EPILOGUE

Lily walked into Quantico, feeling like an entire lifetime had passed since she'd walked through these halls and talked to Director Davy and Chief Brock. There was something bittersweet about returning, although now that she was back in America, Lily longed for the Caribbean sun more than anything. She hadn't heard back from her parents yet, but she was optimistic. Optimistic she could see them again.

She made her way to Chief Brock's office and knocked.

"Come in," her boss called.

Lily opened the door. She could see Chief Brock sitting at his desk, and he looked up at her with a bright smile that contrasted with his dark skin.

"Good morning, Chief Brock," Lily said. "I'm back."

"Ah," Chief Brock said, a slight smile on his face. "Agent Dawn. You have a tan."

They both smiled, and Chief Brock stood up to give Lily a light hug. They'd always had a friendly relationship, and Lily appreciated that. She sat down in front of his desk while he took his rightful spot behind it and clasped his hands together.

"Well, Agent Dawn, I hear great things about your work in Freeport," he said. "Agent Jackson had nothing but good things to say about you."

"You talked to him?" Lily asked.

"Of course. I had to know how you were faring, and I'm not surprised to hear you cracked the case quickly."

Lily smiled and nodded. "Agent Jackson grew on me. He's a good guy underneath all that attitude."

Chief smiled. "That's the spirit."

A pause hung in the air between them. Lily wasn't sure what to say. Then, Chief Brock said something that she was truly not prepared for:

"Lily, you know we love having you here at Quantico," he started.

Lily nodded, listening intently, unsure where he was going with this.

"But . . . the south is where you belong, isn't it?"

Lily was dumbfounded. "Sir?" What was he getting at?

The chief smiled, leaning back in his chair. "Agent Dawn, I want to offer you a permeant transfer. Florida division. With Agent Jackson as your permanent partner."

Lily was gobsmacked, and she sat up straight. "What?"

"Agent Dawn, I'm not going to lie. I've heard about how things went with Agent Jackson in the beginning, and how he treated you. That man needs someone like you to show him what's what." Chief Brock bit his lip, as if he were choosing his next words carefully. "I've worked with you for years, Lily. I've watched you grow. You're great at your job, but Florida—they need more agents down there, and I think a sunny state like that would be perfect for you."

Lily didn't know what to say. Transferring to Florida would be a dream. But she would be saying goodbye to her apartment and to Quantico.

She had so many memories here. This was where she'd spent most of her time as an FBI agent. It was dreary in Virginia sometimes, but in some ways, Lily did like it here.

"Just remember, it's an offer," Chief Brock said, seemingly reading her mind. "Think about it. You'll have opportunities down there you would never get up here."

"Thank you for thinking about me, Chief Brock," Lily said, standing. "I'll definitely think about it."

"Good," he said. He looked happy, and as Lily walked out of his office, she couldn't help but feel elated. Something about this entire case had felt like a shift in the right direction for her career. As Lily left Quantico, she looked back at the building, nostalgia tugging at her heart.

As much as she had appreciated her time here, maybe this was all a sign. Visiting the Caribbean, talking to her father, the dreams of Kara . . .
.

Maybe it meant something.

As she walked toward her car, another thought bloomed in her mind. Maybe it was crazy, but Lily thought that if she did take the job in Florida, she'd be that much closer to Aruba.

She'd be that much closer to where Kara had disappeared.

And maybe, just maybe . . . if she was there . . .

She could investigate Kara's disappearance again. This time, on her own terms. This time, not as Kara's sister—

But as a federal agent.

STILL HOPE
(A Lily Dawn FBI Suspense Thriller —Book 2)

FBI BAU Special Agent Lily Dawn, half Dutch, half Hispanic, raised in the Caribbean, knows the isles like the back of her hand. When a surge in serial killers in the region prods the FBI to assemble a task force, Lily is the natural choice. But Lily is reluctant to face the demons of her past, including her missing sister, and when a new serial killer strikes, leaving victims on a series of remote islands, Lily gears up for a deadly game of cat and mouse.

"The plot has many twists and turns, but it is the ending, which I did not see coming at all, that totally defines this book as one of the most riveting that I have read in years."
—Reader review for Not Like Us

STILL HOPE is book #2 in a long-anticipated new series by #1 bestseller Ava Strong, whose bestseller NOT LIKE US (a free download) has received over 1,000 five star ratings and reviews.

Lily Dawn is called back to the Caribbean. But this is not a happy homecoming. She hasn't seen her parents since moving to Miami ten years ago, and now her sister has been declared legally dead.

Will Lily be able to map out the killer's twisted mind?

A complex psychological crime thriller full of twists and turns and packed with heart-pounding suspense, the LILY DAWN mystery series will make you fall in love with a brilliant new female protagonist and keep you turning pages late into the night.

Future books in the series are now available!

Ava Strong

Ava Strong is author of the REMI LAURENT mystery series, comprising six books (and counting); of the ILSE BECK mystery series, comprising seven books (and counting); of the STELLA FALL psychological suspense thriller series, comprising six books (and counting); of the DAKOTA STEELE FBI suspense thriller series, comprising six books (and counting); and of the LILY DAWN suspense thriller series, comprising five books (and counting).

An avid reader and lifelong fan of the mystery and thriller genres, Ava loves to hear from you, so please feel free to visit www.avastrongauthor.com to learn more and stay in touch.

BOOKS BY AVA STRONG

LILY DAWN FBI SUSPENSE THRILLER
STILL ALIVE (Book #1)
STILL HOPE (Book #2)
STILL AWAKE (Book #3)
STILL HERE (Book #4)
STILL MAD (Book #5)

REMI LAURENT FBI SUSPENSE THRILLER
THE DEATH CODE (Book #1)
THE MURDER CODE (Book #2)
THE MALICE CODE (Book #3)
THE VENGEANCE CODE (Book #4)
THE DECEPTION CODE (Book #5)
THE SEDUCTION CODE (Book #6)

ILSE BECK FBI SUSPENSE THRILLER
NOT LIKE US (Book #1)
NOT LIKE HE SEEMED (Book #2)
NOT LIKE YESTERDAY (Book #3)
NOT LIKE THIS (Book #4)
NOT LIKE SHE THOUGHT (Book #5)
NOT LIKE BEFORE (Book #6)
NOT LIKE NORMAL (Book #7)

STELLA FALL PSYCHOLOGICAL SUSPENSE THRILLER
HIS OTHER WIFE (Book #1)
HIS OTHER LIE (Book #2)
HIS OTHER SECRET (Book #3)
HIS OTHER MISTRESS (Book #4)
HIS OTHER LIFE (Book #5)
HIS OTHER TRUTH (Book #6)

DAKOTA STEELE FBI SUSPENSE THRILLER
WITHOUT MERCY (Book #1)
WITHOUT REMORSE (Book #2)
WITHOUT A PAST (Book #3)
WITHOUT PITY (Book #4)
WITHOUT HOPE (Book #5)

Printed in Dunstable, United Kingdom

69075991R00088